The Elemite Series: Book 1

Changed

Taylor N. Francis

PublishAmerica
Baltimore

First printing

Hardcover 9781462675258
PUBLISHED BY PUBLISHAMERICA, LLLP
www.publishamerica.com
Baltimore

Printed in the United States of America

For my mom, who read the story first.

Acknowledgements

There are so many people I would like to thank for helping me finish my first book. It was such a miracle that I was able to do this and I would never have been able to do it without the help of so many wonderful people.

First of all, I would like to thank my family who supported me in my decision to become a writer. I want to give a special thanks to my parents for helping me make important decisions in my career. Thank you guys for always helping me out and looking out for me. To my brother Austin I would like to say thanks for always being there for me and for being such a great example. I've always admired you and looked up to you. Sydney, thanks for being my best friend and my sister and for inspiring a few of the characters in this book. To my little sister Ryann I would like to say thanks for never giving up on your dreams because that helped me to hang onto mine. I want you to know that I believe in you! I would also like to give a shout out to my little brother Liam for having such a wonderful imagination. Don't ever let anyone try and take that away from you, Liam!

Jessica, thanks for being my other best friend and an awesome cousin. You always encouraged me and helped motivate me. Cherie, you were always so enthusiastic whenever I would talk to you about *Changed* and I would like to thank you for that. You were always cheering me on. I would also like to say thanks to all my other friends who supported me and encouraged me.

Of course I would also like to thank all the wonderful people at PublishAmerica who made all of this possible. I wouldn't have been able to do it without them. Also, I would like to thank the reader for choosing to read my book. I wouldn't be where I am without you. I love you all!

Most of all, I would like to thank my Heavenly Father and His Son, my Lord and Savior Jesus Christ, for giving me this opportunity to live my dream and for helping me out every step of the way. I wouldn't be the person I am today without their help.

Prologue

My mom was right. One moment *can* make a difference. It can change everything. One moment, I'm enjoying my senior year of high school and the next I'm defending myself from a horrible monster. My whole life was changed in just one instant. If I had blinked, I would have missed it.

I looked into the eyes of the blood-thirsty monster before me. This was just between me and him. I knew how I *wanted* it to end—with him gone and everyone I loved left alive—I just didn't know how it was *going* to end. Besides, I wasn't just fighting for my own life; I was fighting for someone so much more important to me than that. If I lost him, I lost my will to live—especially if I could have prevented it. My heart thudded wildly in my chest and my palms were sweaty. As I stood, desperately searching for a weakness in his defenses, I found myself wondering, why me? Why does it have to be me?

Time seemed to move slower and slower as we stared each other down, cautiously waiting for the other to lower their defenses. It was as if time was purposefully creeping along, just so I could be driven insane with the suspense. In reality it was probably only a few seconds, but it felt like an eternity. The atmosphere was so tense that I could almost feel it pressing in around me. Then, finally, he made a decision. He had either decided that he knew where my weak spot was, or he was tired of waiting and was going to try to kill me anyways. He started to make a lunge for my throat. In another moment, I realized that I had less than a second to react. To defend myself…

Chapter 1

Dreams

I woke with a start for the fifth night in a row from the same exact dream. It just felt so *real*. I couldn't just let it go. It had been lingering in my mind for days now. The setting in my dream was very familiar. I knew exactly where it was and how to get there. The problem was that I couldn't figure it out.

I was walking through the forest looking for something, but I had absolutely no idea what it was. I just knew that it was extremely important for me to find it. Suddenly, I felt the need to start running. I took off into the trees like I was being chased. I was running frantically, completely unaware of what was chasing me, but too terrified to look behind me and see what it was. I saw a light up ahead and I knew that if I made it to that light, I'd finally find what I was looking for. And I knew that if I found what I was looking for, it would keep me safe from whatever hideous thing was chasing me. I started to run faster, trying desperately to make it to the light. It was only a few small feet away. I was so close that I started feeling the relief before I even got there.

And I'd always wake up just before I entered the light. It was so frustrating because I knew that this was more than just another ordinary dream. I knew that it meant something. Something extremely important. Like life or death important. Well, maybe not that important. But I wasn't sure. It *could* be a life or death situation.

I went into the bathroom and tried to brush the gigantic snarls out of my long brown hair. When I finally succeeded,

I trotted down the stairs to pour myself a bowl of Frosted Cheerios for breakfast. A quick glance at the calendar told me it was August 20th. I looked out the kitchen window. My mom had apparently already left for work because her car wasn't in the driveway. My little brother Collin was over at a friend's house and my little sister Tracy was at a sleepover, so I had the entire house to myself. But I couldn't just stay in the house. The urge to go was almost overwhelming. I needed to go to that place in the woods. I knew exactly where it was, even though I hadn't been there in so long. I could have found it in my sleep. I used to play there with my dad when I was a little kid. There was something extremely important about that spot and I *really* needed to find out what it was.

I finished my breakfast quickly, scarfing down my cereal as fast as I could without making a mess. I quickly rinsed out my bowl and spoon in the sink and sprinted up the stairs two at a time, nearly tripping over my own feet in the process. I felt like I was in a race as I changed out of my pajamas, brushed my teeth, and dug up my raincoat before sprinting back down the stairs to pack a sack lunch for myself. I wrapped a tuna sandwich in tinfoil and stuffed it in a paper bag with some chips and a soda before bolting out the door to my car.

It was pouring rain as I walked down the driveway to my car. I pulled up my hood and folded my arms over my chest to stay warmer. I wasn't exactly sure what kind of car I had. I didn't speak car. I just knew that it was a used gray Ford of some kind. It was very generic. My mom's car was an old station wagon.

I drove down the familiar dirt road to my favorite spot in the woods. I loved that spot. Well, I loved it and hated it. Sometimes the memories of my dad were a little too much for me to handle. The place was just outside of Sandy, Oregon where I lived. Population: about 12,000 people. The forest was very green with thick vegetation. I loved the way the sunlight looked when it filtered through the trees while the wind swayed the branches, making patterns on the grass with the shadows of the leaves.

But right now I couldn't see the sun. It was raining. There was only one good thing about rain and that was the way the grass smelled when the rain stopped. It was a nice, fresh, spring smell.

As I approached the turn off, the place brought back vivid memories of me and my dad. I was glad that no one was here to see me when I started crying. I took a deep breath then got out of the car and started walking up the small hill that stood between the road and the clearing.

It was a small clearing ringed with trees. When I went there, there was always a carpet of fresh green grass at my feet except in the wintertime. It was a cozy place away from the world where, as a child, I could relax and spend quality time with my dad. I took a deep breath and tried to focus on what I came here for. In my dream, I had been walking through the trees at the edge of the clearing.

I didn't have the slightest clue as to what I was looking for. Nevertheless, I sloshed through the rain looking for whatever-it-was anyway. I was beginning to doubt myself after a little while because in my dream, it wasn't raining. I was debating whether or not I should head back home and wait for a sunnier day, but it started slowly clearing up and after about half an hour, the rain stopped falling altogether.

The thick blanket of clouds remained in the sky. It was as if they were protecting me from who—or what—was going to chase me. That is, *if* my dream was supposed to come true. I walked in circles for hours before getting hungry. It was a good thing that I had thought to bring a lunch. I decided that after I finished eating my lunch I would leave. For all I knew I could be wrong about the dream.

I sat down on a log and pulled the tuna sandwich out of my bag. I unwrapped it and prepared to eat it when suddenly the leaves rustled and a twig snapped. I reflexively looked up towards the source of the noise. What I saw made me freeze with my mouth hanging open and my sandwich halfway to my mouth. Standing not ten feet away from me was an enormous black bear.

My first instinct was to run, but my legs were lead. My eyes were wide and my heart was pumping. My breathing was on the verge of hyperventilation. I decided to stay still and wait to see if it would go away. Maybe it didn't notice me. But all my hopes were crushed when the bear looked right at me and started sniffing the air noisily. My heart started pumping faster and my palms started to sweat.

A thought came into my mind and I realized that the bear probably just wanted the sandwich. I chucked the sandwich as hard and as far as I possibly could and then took off running in the opposite direction. It only worked for about ten seconds. He found and finished the sandwich quickly and then decided to come after me when he was done. I ran as fast I could, but I could feel myself slowly getting tired. My lungs were burning and my legs were aching. My pace started to slacken by an almost undetectable amount. The sun came out of the clouds just then, lighting the way ahead, looking just like it had in my dream. I glanced up at the little halo of blue sky that was showing around the sun.

And then I tripped.

This was just wonderful. Stupid tree root. It's just like my feet to fail me when I needed them most. I should have known this was coming.

The bear approached me and rose up onto its hind legs. It raised one of its massive paws to strike. I squeezed my eyes shut and shielded my face with my arm, waiting. I hoped it would be quick with very little pain. I definitely didn't want my death to be painful. I thought about Mom and Collin and Tracy. If I died, then they would have lost two family members to a bear attack and the news would probably break their hearts.

I almost started crying, but the strike never came. I peeked out from under my arm and almost couldn't believe what I was seeing. There was a guy, about my age, standing between me and the bear. It looked like he was staring at it and concentrating, but I couldn't be sure because he was facing away from me. Then I noticed what the bear was doing. He was acting strangely, backing away from the boy on all fours before finally turning and running away. The boy turned to look at me then. He had a small smile on his face and then another expression flashed across his face, too quickly for me to accurately read. Surprise? Pleasure? Understanding? I couldn't quite figure it out.

"Are you alright?" he asked in a very smooth, appealing voice. I could only imagine the blank expression I had on my face as I stared into his blue eyes. I opened my mouth to speak and when I found out that I couldn't make a sound, I just shut it again and managed to nod. He smiled at me. It was a breathtaking smile that looked like it should be in an advertisement for toothpaste. His hair was shaggy and brown, but not *too* shaggy. His eyes were a beautiful sky blue and his features were as close to perfect as I'd ever seen. He offered me his hand to help me up and when I took it I realized how toned his muscles were. Then something shiny caught my eye and I noticed that he was wearing a necklace with a round onyx charm that had topaz stones embedded in it to make the shape of a paw print.

"Umm," I started when I found my voice again. "Who are you?" I hoped I wasn't being rude.

"I'm Sam Campton," he answered, holding out his hand for a handshake. I took it and decided that he didn't sound offended at my question, so I relaxed.

"Christa McCalliston. Uh, how did you do that?" I asked. He furrowed his eyebrows, looking confused.

"Do what?" he asked innocently. No way. He had to be kidding.

"What you did with the bear," I explained. "All you had to do was stare at it or something. What did you do?" I realized that I probably sounded like an idiot and that I should be thanking him, not accusing him, but I was too curious.

"I'll explain later."

"Do you promise?"

"I promise," he answered solemnly. And strangely, I believed him. He started to walk away.

"Um, Sam?" I called. He stopped and turned to look at me.

"Yeah?"

"Thank you. For saving my life."

He flashed me another brilliant smile. "Anytime," he answered.

"So I'll see you around?"

"Probably." He walked off into the woods leaving me full of questions.

School was starting soon and, even though I was going to start my senior year in high school, I couldn't concentrate on anything but Sam. I sat on my bed staring at the blue lace curtains on my window and tried to figure out who—or what—he was. Maybe he was a hypnotist. That didn't seem likely. Maybe he was some kind of animal trainer. That one didn't seem very likely either. He could be a magician or something. No. That idea was stupider than all my other ideas combined. Maybe he was an alien. No, he wasn't. Well… maybe. Strangely, that one was the most likely explanation to me.

Just then I heard a knock on my door.

"Come in," I said.

"Hey sweetie," my mom said. "Do you want any dinner?"

"Sure." I walked downstairs to the kitchen with my mom. She was a little bit shorter than me with brown hair that went a few inches past her shoulders and big brown eyes. Her face was just a little rounded with rosy cheeks and a perfectly straight and angled nose. She looked pretty good and in shape for a thirty-nine year old. My hair and eye color were the only things I inherited from her.

I sat down at our small kitchen table where a plate of chicken, rice, and veggies was waiting for me. I suddenly realized that I was ravenously hungry. It was probably because that stupid bear stole the sandwich I was going to eat for lunch.

"Thanks, Mom," I told her.

"So how was your day today?"

"Good." My lie came out smoothly. I was surprised. I usually wasn't a terrific liar. "I spent the day just hanging around the house. You know, reading books and doing nothing in particular. So did you have a good day at the bank today?" My mom had worked at the same bank for almost twelve whole years.

"Slow," she answered. "Not too many people get paid on Wednesday. How was your day Tracy?"

"It was great. Stephanie's sleepover was amazing. We watched some movies and ate three pizzas. By ourselves!

You wouldn't believe how many slices I shoveled in. Oh, and today we played volleyball in her backyard. Laura and I beat Stephanie and Sarah by two points."

I was jealous of my sister. It wasn't her looks I was jealous of. She looked a lot like me. The only real differences in our looks was that she was more tan, I had our dad's nose, she had our mom's nose, she was fifteen, and she kept her hair a couple of inches shorter than I did. Her looks weren't the reason I was jealous. I was jealous because she could actually do sports without injuring every other person on the team. And not only was she *able* to play sports, but she was *good* at sports, too. It wasn't fair.

"How was your day, Collin?" my mother asked.

"It was great! Brandon rented that new horror movie *The Stroke of Midnight* – "

"Wait," my mom interrupted. "What's it rated?"

"PG 13. You can even ask Brandon's mom. She knew we were watching it and was perfectly fine with it."

"Ok, go ahead." I tuned out the rest of my little brother's story. I didn't really care about horror movies. Collin had short brown hair and brown eyes. He was going into the eighth grade and he was obsessed with horror movies. Vampires, werewolves, zombies, ghosts, blood, suspense, mystery. You name it. It got kind of tiresome sometimes. I couldn't really complain though. For a little brother, he was oddly non-annoying. Just a little bit too talkative sometimes.

Sam starred in my dreams every night until school started. In each of my dreams, he was something different. A super hero, an alien, a hypnotist. They were all kind of silly, but I still wondered about each of them. I also thought about the dream. The thing that I was looking for was apparently Sam.

The thing that was chasing me was the bear. The part with the light came true, too. So I was right about the dream all along. Now the only thing left to do was to figure out why it was so important and what Sam had to do with anything.

Maybe Sam had an important message for me that would save my life. Maybe I would learn a life lesson because of something he did. Maybe he was supposed to give me something that I would need in the future. Or maybe...we were destined to be together. There were too many possibilities. How was I supposed to know which one it was? What was I supposed to do now? And then there was the way he got the bear to leave. How did he do that? And what exactly did he *do*? It seemed to me like all he did was stand between me and the bear and the bear just decided to turn around and leave. I was certain that the answers to the questions about the bear would give me the answers to all the other questions. And apparently this was a question that would only be answered by asking him myself.

On Sunday night, I had a very different dream.

I was floating, floating out in the open ocean with thousands of tiny fish surrounding me. Hundreds of types and kinds of fish were darting in and out of seaweed, anemones, and coral reefs. It was beautiful and I didn't even feel the need to breath. It was like I could breathe under water. Then the scene changed and I was in the forest, but not a part I recognized, and I was hugging a big black bear. His fur was warm and, for some odd reason, I wasn't scared of him. Then I was lying out on the grass in a big field, letting the sun warm my skin. It felt warm and nice and I could have laid there for hours, drinking in the sunlight. Suddenly I was flying. I was soaring with the birds, twirling and whirling through the clouds, more free than I've ever felt before. The picture changed and I was suddenly planting some seeds in my backyard. I dropped each one carefully into their hole and covered them back up again. After they were planted, I stepped back and watched as they suddenly grew into three giant sunflowers.

I opened my eyes and realized that I was back on my bed in my room. I sat up and looked at the clock on my nightstand. It was only one o'clock in the morning. I sighed and fell back down with my head on the pillow. I closed my eyes and hoped to fall asleep and have that dream again. It was a pretty nice dream. I liked the feeling when I was flying. And when the sun was warming my skin it felt good, too. And floating. Eventually I sunk back into sleep, but it was a disappointing dreamless sleep.

Chapter 2

First Day

I woke up on Monday, August 31st and was suddenly in a much better mood. I was in more than just a better mood. I was elated. I was completely giddy with eagerness. All of the annoyance and irritation that I had felt the past couple of weeks almost completely vanished. One reason was that I started my senior year of high school today, but the more important reason was that Sam would probably be at school and I would most likely run into him. Somewhere in the back of my mind, I realized that I was a little bit too excited at the thought of that, but the other part of my mind didn't really care.

The sun was shining through my blue curtains giving the computer on my desk a bluish tint. I smiled. I couldn't *not* smile. I was glad the sun was shining. It felt good when it warmed my skin. It was so bright and cheerful. It made me even happier than I already was.

I got up quickly and went to turn my light on. Just before I flipped the switch, the light turned itself on. My eyebrows scrunched together in confusion. That was weird. I flipped the switch a couple of times and the lights turned on and off. Just like normal. Everything seemed to be working perfectly fine. Huh. I tried to tell myself that it must have been just my imagination, but something else told me that I didn't imagine it. I ignored it anyways and skipped downstairs for breakfast.

I poured myself a bowl of cereal and sat down at the table to eat it. I thought about my dream while I was eating. It was amazing. I knew that it could never be real in a million years, but it felt like I was actually doing those things. The warm, soft, fur of the bear…the wind in my face as I flew. They couldn't be real, but at the same time, they couldn't be just a dream. Unlike my last strangely real dream, I didn't feel the need to go and fulfill it. Instead, I kept it in the back of my mind for future reference. The bear part did confuse me though. I hated bears. Why was I hugging one?

"Hey, Christa." Tracy had just walked in wearing fuzzy slippers and rubbing her eyes sleepily.

"Oh, hey Trace."

"Can I borrow your blue shirt?" she asked. "The one with the lace at the bottom? And your green belt, too?"

"Sure, go ahead." She grabbed a granola bar from the pantry and then skipped off upstairs to go retrieve my shirt. Apparently I wasn't the only one who was in a happy mood even though school was starting.

And then I saw Collin come thumping down the stairs. It looked like he was still half asleep. I could tell that he was most definitely not at all excited about school. His hair was sticking up in every possible direction and he did not have a happy expression on his face. I almost laughed. His mood was so much different from mine it was almost comical. He popped some pop-tarts in the toaster and glared at it while he waited for them to come up.

My mom rushed down the stairs just then, in a hurry to get to work.

"Can you drive your brother and sister to school, Christa?" she asked while putting on her shoes. "I'm running a little late."

"Sure thing Mom. Have a good day at work."

"You too, honey, bye!" And she was gone.

I finished my cereal and went to go rinse out my bowl in the sink. The faucet turned on before I even touched it. That was weird. What was up today? First the lights, now the faucet? What next? I turned the handle a couple of times and the water pressure changed accordingly. It seemed to be working fine, but I was sure it wasn't my imagination. Were we having electricity *and* plumbing problems? I decided to wait and if this kept up I'd tell Mom so she could call in a professional.

After breakfast, I went upstairs to get dressed for school. I pulled on my favorite pair of jeans with a white shirt and a gray cardigan. I combed all of the knots out of my tangled hair and thought about putting it up in a ponytail, but decided against it.

Instead of listening to Tracy babble on and on, I let my mind wander as I drove to school. I wondered idly if I'd have any classes with Sam or if I'd have to talk to him at lunch. There was a pretty good chance that he was going to be in at least *one* of my classes. At least, that's what I was hoping. There were about 350 students in my senior class and 1,400 in the entire high school. There were about 4,200 in the entire school district. Oregon Trail School District covers Sandy, Boring, and the Mt. Hood area. There are six elementary schools, three middle schools and one high school. But in Sandy itself, there's only one of each.

I dropped Collin off at Cedar Ridge Middle School first. He still wasn't happy about the whole back-to-school thing. He dragged his feet as he walked away.

I pulled into the parking lot at the high school where Tracy and I would be starting our sophomore and senior years. Our high school was the home of the Pioneers. Some people were wearing red and black, our school colors, but most weren't. Tracy took out her schedule.

"Hey, do you know where Mr. Carl's room is?" she asked.

"Yeah. Just go through that door and take a left. It's the third door on the right. You can't miss it. He has a big sign on the door."

"Thanks Christa." She walked away and I took out my schedule. Spanish II was my first class. I walked into class and immediately scanned the room for Sam. He wasn't there. The rest of first period went by in a daze. It wasn't hard to tune out grey-haired Señor Gonzales rambling on about our goals for the year and what his expectations were.

After class I looked at my schedule again. Second period was English. I looked for Sam again when I entered the class, but he wasn't in this class either. I listened to Ms. Thomas long enough to find out the list of novels we would be reading and then I tuned her out, too. I looked at my schedule and saw that I only had one more class before lunch. It was history. This was it. If he wasn't in my history class, I'd have to talk to him at lunch.

When I walked into the room, I realized that this was the opportunity I was looking for. He was in my history class and there was an empty seat right next to him. I hurried to sit down.

"O.K. Sam," I said. "Can you explain now?" This is what I'd been waiting this whole time for. I was ready for any response he gave me. I wasn't going to laugh. I wasn't going to be mad. I just wanted to know what he did to the bear.

"Can we at least get to know each other and be friends first? Because at the moment we're almost complete strangers."

"Umm…Okay." That took me off guard. "What do you want to know?"

"Well, um, let's see. What's your favorite food?"

"Tuna melts," I said with a smile.

"If you could live anywhere in the world, where would it be?"

"Here."

"Why?"

"It's home," I answered simply. He asked a few more questions before starting to dig in a little deeper.

"So, um, you live with your mom," he stated.

"That's not a question," I answered. He waited. I sighed. "Yes, I live with my mom."

"And what happened to your dad?"

"He, umm," I hesitated and looked down at my hands.

"Sorry if that's too personal," he said quickly, trying to apologize. "You don't have to answer if you don't want to." We sat in silence for another moment.

"He passed away when I was eleven," I answered finally. I kept my eyes on my hands, hoping I wouldn't start crying.

"I'm sorry," he said softly.

I looked up at him then. His eyes were apologetic as he watched me.

"What about you?" I asked. It was probably a good idea to change the subject before the tears spilled over. He didn't seem at all surprised that I changed the subject. I could tell he understood.

"I live with my brother and sisters, my brother-in-law, and my grandfather." We started to whisper because class had begun. Mr. Robinson didn't seem to notice that we were still talking. We weren't the only ones, anyways. Most of the class was still whispering to each other.

"Tell me about them."

"My sister, Tasha, is twenty-two. She just opened her own flower shop. My brother, Brian, is a junior and wants to be a pilot. My adopted sister, Chelsea, is also a junior and was the head of the girls' varsity swim team at our old school. Tasha recently got married to a guy named Kyle. Kyle is twenty-three and just got a job as a chef at one of those fancy restaurants. We all help each other take care of Grandpa George. He's getting quite old. Seventy-six to be exact. But that's enough about me and my family. I want to know about *you*." I braced myself. What kind of question was he going to ask this time?

"Wait, one more question." He waited patiently. "What happened to your parents?"

"They died a long time ago," he said sadly. "My brother, sister and I were put up for adoption, but my sister, who was fourteen at the time, made sure we didn't get adopted. She wanted us to stay together. So she promised that we'd all be adopted together, or she'd adopt us herself as soon as she turned eighteen. The adoption agency found out that we still had a grandfather not long after that. And he adopted Chelsea, too, because Brian had become a little attached to her." He chuckled to himself.

"So, where exactly did you move from?"

"New York City."

"Wow, that's so cool. Big change, huh?"

"Yeah, tell me about it. Now can I ask *you* some more questions?"

"Go ahead," I told him. "Ask me anything." Well, maybe not *anything*, I added on mentally. Why did I have to be so stupid? I shouldn't have given him the power to ask me anything. I scolded myself and promised to do better at that.

"Do you have any siblings?"

"My sister Tracy is fifteen and she just started driver's ed. last weekend. She's in to sports and is a really good athlete. My brother Collin is thirteen and he's really in to horror movies. He can't get enough of them. Any more questions?"

"What's your favorite color?" That took me off guard. I was expecting another really personal question. I guess he forgot to ask a couple of not-so-deep questions and decided to come back to them.

"Blue," I answered automatically.

"What's your favorite type of music?"

"Pop. Or rock. But not the screaming kind of rock, the good kind. Country can be good, too." His questions continued like that as we walked into the lunchroom and he kept them coming all the way until the end of lunch. He would have kept going, but we didn't have our next class together. He had calculus and I had study hall.

On my way to fourth period study hall, I realized that I hadn't gotten the information that I had been waiting this entire time for. He hadn't explained a thing! I walked into class mad at myself for letting him distract me like that. He tricked me and I fell for it. I sat down and put my chin on my arms. I heard someone sit down in the desk next to me, but whoever it was left me alone.

It was all too easy to tune out Mrs. Wilhelm's lecture about study hall rules. I couldn't have focused if I tried. I was too angry with myself. How could I have wasted a perfect opportunity like the one I was given? Fifth period was art with Mrs. Brown and sixth was physics with Mr. Dexter. They both went by quickly. I didn't pay any attention to them at all.

Tracy was waiting for me by the car after school. She was already talking before I was even within earshot. On our way home from school, I thought about the interrogation Sam had given me and how he had so easily distracted me. I would get the answers I wanted out of him tomorrow. He wouldn't distract me this time. I picked up Collin from school and he seemed to be in a better mood. It was like Collin and I had swapped moods from this morning.

I went inside and put my school bag away. Then I plopped down on my bed and picked up my iPod. I plugged it into the speaker and pressed play, not caring which song came on. I laid my head down on my pillow and tried to relax. I tried to make it so there was only one thing I was thinking about. And that was not thinking.

I don't know when or how I fell asleep, but I woke with a start to find my mom's face about a foot from mine. She had shaken me lightly and that's what had woken me up.

"Christa, honey," she said gently, "did you want any dinner?"

"Sure, Mom. I'll be down in a minute." She gave me a small smile and walked back out the door, closing it behind her. I got up slowly and turned my iPod off, then headed to the bathroom to see what I looked like. My hair was a haystack. There was no way these knots were going to come out. Ever. I sighed and did my best to comb through the mess. After I decided that it was tamed enough to hide in a ponytail, I left the bathroom to go eat. I trotted down the stairs, my brown ponytail bobbing behind me.

The next morning, I looked out my window and groaned. It was foggy outside, which would make it much harder to see the road. The ride to school was going to be a nightmare. I couldn't see more than a couple of inches out the window. I wished the fog would just go away. It was unwelcome here. The last thing I needed was to crash. Then, to my utter amazement, it started clearing up. My mood lifted drastically as I drove myself and my little siblings to school. I hated fog and was glad to be rid of it.

Chapter 3

Rachel

I walked into history class determined to get some answers. I wouldn't get distracted and I wouldn't let him change the subject. I'd been thinking about it all morning.

"Are you going to explain now? I've been waiting and it's been driving me crazy." I figured that it was time Sam started explaining, so I asked him the question before I was even all the way seated. He sighed. I watched his face carefully, trying to decipher his reaction. I wasn't sure, but I thought he looked a little annoyed and exasperated but also slightly amused at the same time.

"How about at lunch?" he asked.

"Why can't you explain here?"

"Because we're in class."

"Good point," I allowed. "Do you promise that you'll explain?"

"I promise."

"No more interrogations?"

"No more interrogations," he laughed.

I was walking beside him on our way to lunch when I heard my name being called. I reflexively looked around until I spotted the person who had called to me. A humongous grin spread across my face. It was the person I'd been missing this whole summer. My best friend through thick and thin. She was a couple of inches shorter than me with shoulder length brown hair and side bangs. Her skin was mildly tan and her cheeks were rosy. I noticed that she was wearing her favorite pair of jeans. I had given them to her as a gift for her birthday several months ago.

"Oh my gosh! Rachel!" I said as she ran towards me, completely ecstatic. This was a total surprise. I ran over to meet her. "I thought you said you were going to miss the second day of school, too!" We had our fingers locked together and we were squealing and jumping up and down like a couple of little kids. I was so excited to see her, I felt like screaming.

"Yeah, I was, but then Great Grandma Meredith found out that I was missing two days of school to see her, so she sent me home on an airplane right away." She rolled her eyes. Rachel had gone to see her Great Grandma in Pittsburg and was gone all summer. I was left here, feeling completely abandoned. "She's such a crazy old woman. There's no work you have to make up for from the first two days of school. There might be a couple of lists of expectations and syllabuses that they hand out, but other than that…" She was shaking her head as she trailed off.

"I missed you so much," I said as I hugged her as tight as I could.

"I missed you, too, Christa," she replied, hugging me back. "Anyways, it's good to be back home in good old Sandy, Oregon," she said as she pulled back and spread out her arms, gesturing to everything around her. Suddenly, she stopped. She was staring past me, over my shoulder at something behind me. I turned my head to follow her stare, confused. Oh. So she had noticed Sam.

"Who's this?" she asked.

"This is Sam," I said, gesturing to him with my hand. "Sam, Rachel. Rachel, Sam."

"Hello," Sam said politely.

"Uh, hi," Rachel said, uncharacteristically shy.

"Excuse us, Sam," I muttered, pulling Rachel by the arm. She had a dazed look on her face as I towed her along.

"Wow!" she exclaimed as soon as we were out of earshot. Her green eyes were bright with excitement. She showed her white teeth as a brilliant smile stretched across her face – almost literally from ear to ear.

"I know, I know," I said.

"Who *is* he?" She jabbed her thumb back over her shoulder towards Sam as she spoke. "I mean, he's like the hottest guy I've ever seen in my life besides guys that are on TV."

"Well," I started. Then I sighed and it all came out in a rush. "He saved me from an attacking bear a couple of weeks ago and we had lunch together yesterday. I really don't know a lot about him." I paused for a second. "But I want to," I added.

"Wow," she repeated. "I'd want to get to know him, too, if I were you. I mean he's hot *and* he rescued you? I wonder if he's single." I rolled my eyes and towed her back over to Sam. I was confused by his amused expression. It was as if he had heard everything we said. I ignored it and we all walked into the lunchroom together. Rachel was staring at Sam the whole time.

I didn't ask Sam to explain all during lunch. I didn't know why, but I felt like the conversation where he explains everything to me should be done with just the two of us, without Rachel there to listen. So instead, I kept Rachel the center of attention by asking her all about her trip to Pittsburg.

"Pittsburg has four very distinct seasons," she was saying. "Most of the time you just hear about how cold it gets in the winter or whatever, but what most people don't know is that it actually gets pretty hot in the summer. At least, hot to me. I spent a lot of my time at the pool.

"It doesn't get as hot as Phoenix, though. I have an uncle who lives in Phoenix. I've been there during the summer and it's not pleasant. We went there last Christmas and it felt like the temperature it gets in spring here in Sandy.

"Great Grandma Meredith and I spent a lot of time in her apartment with the air conditioning running. She told me that it was a lot hotter than usual over there. She showed me how to knit, too. I'll have to show you the scarf I made. I feel like I'm monopolizing the conversation. What did you do over summer vacation, Chris?"

"I got a job at Carson's Convenience Store. The one Matt's dad owns," I answered. "Other than that I didn't do much."

"That's great, Christa! Congrats on the new job. I need a job, too. You know, to earn money for college and stuff. I'm pretty close to broke right now. I'm going to have to start looking for openings…" I listened to everything she had to say. It was kind of funny to listen to her. It was just like Rachel to just keep talking and talking and talking. She talked at a hundred words a minute about almost any subject you could possibly think of.

Rachel and I had study hall together and she talked the whole way there. Only now she wasn't talking about Pittsburg or her need for a job, she was talking about Sam.

"Oh my gosh," she gushed. "He is so hot. And you said he saved your life?"

"Yeah, he saved me from a bear."

"*How?*"

"I don't know," I admitted. "I had my eyes closed."

"Oh well," she answered, shrugging. "It doesn't matter anyways. All that matters is that he saved you. That's good enough for me."

I suddenly felt guilty. She was right. It didn't matter how

he saved me. And here I was bugging him to tell me. I was being annoyingly persistent. And the worst part about it was, even though I felt guilty, I knew I was still going to ask him. I was just going to keep on being annoyingly persistent. And that was really depressing. I must be a pretty horrible person.

Chapter 4

It Just Brought Up More Questions

"Ok," I said to Sam when I took my usual spot in history. "Explain."

"Maybe it will be easier if I demonstrate first," Sam answered.

"Go ahead."

"Let's see if you can turn that light off without touching the switch."

Did I hear him right? Did he seriously just ask me to do that? Who did he think I was? Some kind of psychic or magician or something?

"Is this some kind of joke?"

"I didn't intend it to be. Do you think it's funny?" he answered innocently. I was debating with myself on whether he was being sarcastic or not.

"Ha, ha, very funny. Seriously, though. Just tell me how you did it."

"I told you. You got to try to turn off the lights first."

"This is nuts! I mean, you can't be serious. You're just trying to make me look stupid or something so you can laugh at me."

"I promise that I'm not trying to make you look stupid or anything. Just do it. Turn the light off. Just the one that's directly above us. The others can stay on."

"How am I supposed to do that?"

"Just stare at it and concentrate," he told me. "I need to know something before I can tell you anything."

"Isn't staring at lights bad for your eyes?"

"Not yours. And you won't be staring at it long enough anyway."

"What does that even mean?"

"Just do it."

I wasn't sure if he was serious or not, but I sighed and turned my head to look up at the light anyways. I squinted my eyes, concentrated as hard as I could, and gave it an honest effort. I was about to give up when the light suddenly flicked off. I gasped and the light flicked back on.

"That was good," he said.

"Is this some kind of trick? Do you have a switch or something under the table?" I asked as I bent over to examine the underside of the table and his hands. There wasn't anything there.

"No," he said as I came back up.

"Then it was the luckiest coincidence that I've ever experienced in my life."

"Nope. It wasn't a coincidence."

"So what you're saying is that *I* did that."

"Yep."

"Ha, ha! That's a good one."

"This isn't a joke either."

"If that's true then that must be why the faucet and the lights turned on before I touched them at home, right?" I was only being half serious, but he took it very seriously.

"Wait," he said, suddenly alert. "The faucet *and* the lights?"

"Yeah," I said confused. "Could you keep it down? Class just started."

"Sorry," he whispered. "That just took me by surprise."

"Would you please explain now? I can assure you that I'm way more surprised and confused than you right now."

"Not here," he said.

"Then where?" I was starting to get annoyed. So his plan was to show me that and then make me wait even *longer* before he explained? He was really getting on my nerves.

"Remember that place in the woods?" he asked. "Where we met?"

"Yeah," I said holding back the wave of sadness that washed over me whenever I thought of that spot. I remembered that place alright.

"Let's meet there."

"Ok," I agreed. "When?"

"How about after school?"

"Sounds good."

He paused. "What you said about the faucet and the lights made me curious."

"And?"

"And I wanted to see if you could do something."

"Like what?"

"Let's see if you can make a slight breeze."

"In the classroom?"

"Yeah." I studied his face carefully. I wasn't sure what he was getting at.

"Ok, I'll give it a shot," I told him. I wasn't sure what this had to do with anything, but I decided to try anyways. I closed my eyes and concentrated. I felt my hair brush softly against my face and heard some papers rustle. The breeze felt good. It blew a pleasant scent towards me. It smelled wonderful. I wondered what was making that scent. I inhaled and opened my eyes. As soon as my eyes were opened, I lost my concentration and the breeze stopped. I was feeling a little lightheaded, but nothing too bad. Some students were looking around, obviously confused by the sudden breeze in the classroom. Others were picking up papers that had blown off their desks onto the floor.

"Well done," he congratulated.

"This is getting a little too weird," I answered. "I suppose you're going to tell me that this is the reason the fog cleared up when I wanted it to?"

He thought about it for a second. "Probably."

"You realize that this is just making me more confused."

"I know."

"Just checking."

At lunch I sat with Rachel and some of my other friends who I had neglected the past two days. Jennifer, also known as Jen or Jenny, had shoulder-length curly red hair, brown eyes, and freckles. She was always smiling and friendly. Benjamin, also known as Ben, was average height with blond hair and blue eyes. I wasn't sure, but I thought that he might be developing a crush on me. Matthew, also known as Matt, was a little tall and had brown hair and hazel eyes. He was pretty good looking. I knew that Rachel had a crush on him.

Sam sat with his adopted sister Chelsea and his brother Brian, across the cafeteria from me. I kept stealing glances at them when I was sure no one was looking. Chelsea had wildly curly brown hair and blue eyes. She had a kind face and dimples. Brian was kind of tall with short blond hair and green eyes. He was pretty muscular. I wondered if he worked out or if he was on some kind of sports team or both. They were "the new kids," so every few minutes somebody would come by and introduce themselves to them. The town is small enough that it's a little harder to hide if you're new in town.

Chapter 5

Chelsea

After lunch I walked to the study hall room with Rachel. She chattered the whole time and I listened to every word, laughing with her at all of the ridiculous stories she told. She had the weirdest experiences sometimes.

"So there we were," she was saying. "Sitting on the side of the road in the middle of nowhere with no gas and no cell phone reception. That wasn't even all of it. To top it all off, it was raining. And so we just sat there watching car after car pass by, and none of them even slowed.

"And then, finally a truck-driver stops to help us and guess who it is? It was none other than Chuck, the driver who delivers the merchandise to Carson's Convenience Store. Oh my goodness, we were so glad to see him. I mean, we'd been out there for hours. Anyways, he tows our car to the nearest gas station and helps us out a little bit. All in all, it was a pretty crazy experience. But one thing is for sure, I'm never getting into a car that doesn't have at least half a tank of gas. I'm pretty sure Matt and Jenny feel the same way."

After study hall I made my way down to the art room. When I walked into class I realized that Chelsea had that class with me, so I eagerly claimed the empty seat next to her.

"Hi, I'm Christa," I greeted her when I sat down. "Are you new? I don't remember ever seeing you before. In a small town like this, it's hard to hide it if you're new in school."

"You're right, I am new. It's nice to meet you. I'm Chelsea." I could see a lot of curiosity in her eyes when she looked at me. I wasn't sure why meeting me would make her look at me with that kind of interest. It made me feel self-conscious.

"You must be Sam's sister. He's in my history class."

"That's me."

"So you like art?"

"Yeah," she replied. "It's calming."

"I feel the same way. I can just sit there for hours and forget everything when I'm drawing. I love it. Anyways, Sam tells me that you were the head of the girls' varsity swim team at your old school?"

"That's right. I just love the water."

"I know exactly what you mean," I answered, remembering how it felt to float in my dream. "You know what Chelsea? I think we're going to be great friends."

"I agree."

Just then something caught my eye and I noticed that she was wearing a necklace with a silver chain and a sapphire charm made to look like a drop of water.

"Wow!" I exclaimed. "What's that necklace made out of?"

"Oh, well the chain is silver and the charm is sapphire."

"Really? Its *real* sapphire and silver?

"Yeah."

"Wow," I said again. "It must be worth a fortune."

"I don't know what it's worth as far as money goes, but it's priceless to me."

"Where did you get it?" I asked.

She hesitated, seemingly unsure of what to say. "It was a gift," she answered finally.

"Wow," I said for the third time. "It's so pretty."

I stared at it for another small moment and then focused on the assignment we were given.

I needed something to clear my mind and we were doing the perfect thing in art today. The assignment was a free sketch and Mrs. Brown's directions were pretty simple. Just draw whatever you want.

I took my sketch book and pencil out of my bag and began to draw. I didn't realize what I was drawing until it was all done. The picture I had drawn was a necklace with a circular charm that had a star in the middle with five points. The picture confused me. What had inspired me to draw this? I had never seen it before. It was probably the same thing that inspired me to go into the woods and find out what I was looking for. Maybe it had something to do with whatever Sam was. I had a feeling that there was something extremely important about it. I realized that I was having that feeling a lot lately. Could they all be related? Could they all have something to do with Sam?

I sat by Matt in physics.

"Hey Christa!" he greeted me cheerfully.

"Hey Matt," I muttered, not really listening. I was there physically, but my thoughts were other places. I had too many thoughts floating around in my head.

He seemed to notice that there was a lot on my mind and decided not to bother me for the rest of the period. I was grateful for that. I was still thinking about the drawing I made in art. For some reason, I felt like it was important.

I should have been paying more attention because I had no idea what the lesson was on, which would probably hurt me later since I always struggled to get good grades in any science I've ever taken. I think the highest grade I ever got in a science class was a B+. I honestly tried to pay attention, but I kept getting distracted by other thoughts. The fact that Mr. Dexter's lessons were never very exciting didn't help, either. Science just couldn't hold my attention.

As soon as the final bell rang, I grabbed my stuff and ran out to my car. I threw my stuff in the back and climbed in the front. I waited impatiently for Tracy. When she finally got in the car, I backed out of my parking space and drove out of the parking lot, heading towards Collin's school.

I dropped Tracy and Collin off at home and then drove off towards the woods.

Tears were stinging in my eyes during my drive to our designated spot in the clearing. This place always made me cry. I just couldn't help it. This was the place that I had spent the most time with my dad when he was alive. I thought that after all this time I would be able to handle it a little better. I could handle it, just not here. I tried to suck back my tears and prevent them from spilling over as I drove down the familiar lane that wove through the trees.

Chapter 6

It Just Gets Weirder and Weirder

I arrived at the clearing in the woods with tears in my eyes. I got out of the car and concentrated on stopping the tears from spilling over. It took a couple of deep breaths and a lot of concentration to do that.

"Ok Sam," I said as soon as I saw him. I was impatient to get started. "We're finally alone where we can talk – and more importantly, where you can explain – with no distractions." I had made sure that all of my tears were wiped away before approaching him so that he couldn't see that I'd been crying. I didn't want him asking too many questions.

"Ok, but I have a few more tests for you first."

"You make me sound like a science experiment," I muttered, frowning. He just laughed. I wanted to be annoyed at him for laughing at me, but I couldn't. I loved his laugh too much. It was the most beautiful sound I ever heard. *Snap out of it!* I told myself. I had to concentrate on what he was going to tell me.

"What's the first test?" I asked him.

"See that bird up there?" He pointed to the top of a tall tree. I was surprised when I could see the bird clearly from all the way down here. I nodded and he continued to explain. "See if you can call it down to perch on your finger."

"Why aren't any of your tests, umm, I don't know… normal?!"

He laughed at me again. "Define 'normal'."

"Like not impossible or magical or mystical or whatever."

"Just do it." I was confused by what he had told me to do, but I tried anyways. I held out my finger and started to whistle.

"Not like that!" he nearly shouted. I jumped and looked at him, a startled expression on my face. "With your mind!" He said it as if it were the most obvious thing in the world.

"I'm sorry, I wasn't aware that I had mind powers," I said sarcastically.

"Just try it."

I was a little put out by his rudeness, but I still turned back to look at the bird and started concentrating on getting it to fly down and land on my finger. To my utter amazement, it flew down to me from its branch so it could perch lightly on my outstretched finger.

"Very good," he praised me. He sounded almost as surprised as I felt. It was a little insulting. Why would he be surprised when he's giving the tests? When I turned my head to look at him, the bird flapped its wings and took off. I watched as it flew over the trees and out of sight.

"Any more tests?"

"Don't worry, we're almost done," he assured me. "Follow me over to that puddle over there." He took my hand and started towing me over to the puddle in question. I liked the feel of his hand around mine. It was strong and comforting.

"I don't see how any of these tests have anything to do with each other," I grumbled. "Can't you just explain already? This is getting kind of old and I've been waiting forever for an explanation."

"Don't worry, you'll know soon enough." We reached the puddle just then and he knelt down beside it, being careful to not get any mud on his knees. I copied him.

"Let's see if you can evaporate some of this puddle." I just stared at him blankly. He had to be kidding me. What was all of this about anyways? It didn't make any sense. "You don't have to evaporate the whole thing," he clarified. "Just turn a little bit of it into vapor." I didn't think that it really mattered how much water I had to evaporate. It was still weird. I sighed and turned to the puddle anyways. Unsure of how it was supposed to work, I stretched out my arms so that my hands were over the puddle, palms down. I started to concentrate. I had done so many of these silly tests that it didn't surprise me when the puddle slowly got smaller and the air around me slowly got more humid.

"Are we done now?"

"One more test," he answered. I sighed. He laughed.

"See if you can make that blade of grass grow about half an inch or more."

"Whatever you say," I sighed. I concentrated on the grass and—what a surprise—it grew. "Would you please explain what's going on now? You said that was the last test."

"Ok," he said. "As you have probably already guessed, you're not a normal human. In fact, you're not a human at all. You and I are both Elemites."

"So you're saying that we're both freaks and you can do all of the stuff that I just did?"

"Not all of it," he answered. This confused me. Didn't he just say that he was the same as me? "You see, you're not a normal Elemite either."

"So what you're saying is that I'm a freak among freaks?" I nearly shouted. "Well that's comforting!"

"No," he replied. "You're just more powerful."

"I'm confused."

"Maybe it will be easier if I explain about *normal* Elemites first."

"Probably."

"Ok," he began. "Elemites appear to be normal humans on the outside, but really we have special powers. We have super strength, super speed, super eyesight, super hearing, and a super sense of smell. Each Elemite also has one additional power. Elemites can have power over light and fire, water, plants and earth, air, or animals. For instance, I am an Animal Elemite."

"So is that the difference between me and a normal Elemite?" I asked. "Is it because I have all of the powers?"

"Yeah."

"But *why* am I different?"

"I don't know. You're the first Elemite to ever have control of all the Elements. It's never happened before, at least, not that I know of. Who knows? Maybe you're not the first. All I know is that it's at least extremely rare."

"Then how did you know that you were supposed to test me on all of them after you found out that I could do one? I mean, after you found out I could control light, wouldn't you just assume I was a Light Elemite? What made you think to test me on the others?" I asked all of these questions without room in between for answers. This was all getting a little too weird for me.

"Because you said that the faucet *and* the lights would turn on," he answered. "A Light Elemite can't turn on the faucet and a Water Elemite can't turn on the lights." He shrugged. It seemed pretty obvious to him. I thought about that for a second. Was he saying that I was one of the most powerful beings on the planet? That couldn't be right. How can someone be super powerful *and* super clumsy?

"I think it's time for us both to go." The sound of his voice interrupted my train of thought. "I'm sure I've given you a lot to think about. You'll probably need a little time to let it sink in," he said. "See you tomorrow," he added after a moment, flashing me one of his dazzling smiles.

When I got home, I went inside and put my school bag away. I sat down on my bed and took out the drawing I made in art. I wondered if this had anything to do with Elemites. I was about to put it away and go get a snack when I suddenly felt like there was something hanging around my neck. A necklace? I reached my hand up and, sure enough, I was wearing a necklace. I undid the clasp and took it off to get a better look.

What I saw made me gasp. It was the same symbol that was in my drawing. I compared it again and again and I even slapped myself a couple of times to make sure I wasn't dreaming. But it didn't disappear and it didn't change shape, so it must be real. The circle was silver and the star on the inside was gold. The chain on the necklace was silver like the circle. I wasn't sure, but I thought that it might be made of real gold and silver. I made a mental note to take it to a jeweler in Portland and check. I was going to have to ask Sam if this had anything to do with Elemites. Considering the past couple of weeks, it probably did.

Ben greeted me eagerly when I walked into Spanish. Apparently I had encouraged him by sitting with them at lunch yesterday. I sighed.

"Hey Christa!" he exclaimed. "Mind if I sit by you?"

"No, I don't mind." I didn't want to hurt his feelings. We were still friends.

"Hey, that's a nice necklace you got there."

"Thanks."

"So I was thinking," he began. Uh oh. I hoped he wasn't going to say what I thought he was going to say. "Maybe we could go see a movie and get a bite to eat on Saturday?" Dang it. He said what I thought he was going to say.

"I'm sorry, Ben, but I work on Saturday. I just got a job at Carson's Convenience Store. The one Matt's dad owns." I was suddenly even more grateful for that job than I was before. At least I had a legitimate excuse not to go out with Ben. I didn't have to make up some last minute plans or come up with a lie that he would probably see through.

"Oh, ok," he answered sadly. "Maybe some other time."

"Maybe," I allowed. "Maybe" wasn't a word that guaranteed anything.

Ben didn't say anything for the rest of the class. This was going to get frustrating.

I sat by Jenny in English and she asked me if I wanted to go on a shopping spree with her and Rachel in Portland a week from Friday.

"Maybe. I work on Friday, so I'll see if I can trade shifts with Kenton or Matt." I needed a girl's night out. It was a good distraction.

"Hey where'd you get that necklace?" she asked. "It's really pretty." Oh, so she had noticed it.

"Oh, um," I said. "I just found it."

"You *found* that?" she said astonished. "*Where?*"

"In my bedroom."

"In your *bedroom*? That's weird."

"I know."

"Is it *real* gold and silver?"

"I don't know," I answered. "I'll have to take it to a jeweler in Portland."

"That would be so cool if it was gold and silver."

"No kidding."

Sam was sitting in his usual spot in history.

"I have a question for you."

He looked at me warily before answering. "What's your question?"

"Does this have anything to do with Elemites?" I asked pointing at my necklace.

"Interesting," he said fingering the gold and silver charm.

"Is that all you're going to say?"

Instead of answering, he asked me a question. "Where did you find this?"

"On my neck," I answered. "It just appeared. But it was *after* I drew this." I took my drawing from art class out of my bag and showed it to him.

"Interesting," he repeated as he studied the drawing.

"So?"

"So what?"

"Does it have anything to do with us?" This was getting a little frustrating.

"Of course it does," he said. He was making it sound like it was supposed to be obvious again. He really did drive me crazy sometimes. "It's your symbol."

"My symbol?"

"Yeah," he answered. "Every Elemite has a symbol. This is mine." He pointed to the necklace he was wearing. It was the one that had the paw print. "I was wondering what your sign was going to be," he continued, "since you can control all the Elements. You get your symbol after your powers fully come in. That means that you're capable of doing all the things other Elemites can do, but you haven't necessarily been trained to reach your full potential yet. Your symbol contains all your Elemental powers."

"Elemental powers?"

"Your powers are categorized into two groups: Elemental powers and super human powers. Elemental powers include your power over light, earth, animals, water, and air. An Elemite's super human powers include your super human strength, super speed, super hearing, super eyesight, and your super strong sense of smell. So basically, if you're wearing your symbol necklace, you can use all your powers and if you're not then you can only use your super human powers."

"So if I'm not wearing my necklace I can still pick up a car and hear a pin drop in a loud room, but I can't start a fire with my mind or cause the wind to pick up."

"Right."

"And this is my official symbol?" I asked.

"Yep."

"So is Chelsea a Water Elemite?"

"How'd you guess?"

"It wasn't too hard to figure out," I told him. "She has Water Elemite written all over her. She's your adopted sister, she's the head of the swim team, and she wears a necklace with a charm shaped like a water droplet. I assume that's her symbol?"

"Very good. You're much more observant than I thought."

"You know, I still have a lot of questions. Should we meet in the same place, at the same time as yesterday?"

"Sounds good."

"So did Jenny already ask you about Friday?" Rachel asked me at lunch.

"Yeah, Ray." I smiled. "But I have to find out if I can trade shifts with Matt or something. Hey, Matt!" He looked up when I said his name. "The girls are having a girl's night out on Friday. Is there any way I can trade shifts with you? I'll work on Thursday and you can take my shift on Friday."

"Sure thing, Christa."

"Thanks." Then I turned back to Rachel. "I'm in, Ray."

"Cool. We're going to have so much fun. It'll be great to go to a mall for once. I mean this little town has nothing pretty much. We don't have any good clothing stores. Sandy's great and all, but you got to have more selection..." And she was off. It was typical Rachel and I loved her for it.

Chapter 7

Any Questions?

"You said that you had some questions for me?" Sam asked when I arrived at the infamous spot in the woods.

"Yes."

"Go ahead," he prompted, sitting on the ground. I sat down next to him and tried to think of what I wanted to ask first.

"Alright, um, well, first off, do Elemites have any enemies or anything like that?"

"Only one," he answered sounding amused. Why was this funny? "Vampires."

"Vampires?" Oh, so now Vampires were real, too? Was it ever going to end?

"Vampires are our natural enemies because our blood tastes and smells so much better to them than human blood."

"Well, don't we have ways to protect ourselves from them?" I asked. "Our powers are helpful right? I mean, how do you kill a Vampire?"

"There are a few ways to kill a Vampire," he answered. "Elemites are strong enough to rip them apart, but humans, of course, can't. But tearing them apart does absolutely no good unless you tear off the head, otherwise they can put themselves back together."

"They can *put themselves back together?*" I repeated incredulously.

"Yeah. And killing them is not as easy as it sounds because Vampires can fight back. That's why Elemites have special abilities. Animal Elemites, like me, have to use bears to help us fight back. For some reason, bears are the only animals that can tear a Vampire's skin with its claws."

"Alright, first off, killing Vampires *doesn't* sound easy," I interrupted. "And secondly, why bears? It seems a bit random to me." It was just my luck that the animal that was supposedly the most helpful to me was also the one I hated the most.

"I guess you're right that it doesn't sound easy, but it's still harder than it sounds. And as for your second question, I have no idea."

"Oh, okay, well you can keep on going with what you were saying before. Sorry for interrupting."

"That's alright. Um, anyways, water makes a Vampire as weak as a human in strength, but since it doesn't have a beating heart and blood in its veins, you still have to rip the head off to kill it. That's where the myth about how Vampires can't cross running water came from. Fire can burn Vampires, but it doesn't do much unless you burn the head. And, of course it dies if you burn the head *off*. Or you can burn the whole thing of course. There is only one type of plant in the world that acts as a poison to Vampires, but it doesn't affect humans and it can actually *heal* Elemites. I guess you could call it a 'mythical' plant because it's unknown to humans. Humans mistake it for some sort of exotic South American flower. It's called a Poison Healer. Just touching it will make a Vampire sick and, unless he drinks the blood of a Unicorn, he has 24 hours to live—"

"Wait, Unicorns?" I interrupted.

"Yes, Unicorns. I'll tell you about them in a minute. Can I continue with Vampire weaknesses now?"

"Yeah, sorry."

"If sand gets into a Vampire's eyes, it completely blinds them for about an hour. That's where the Air and Earth

Elemites' powers come in handy. Also, Vampires can't fly, so Air Elemites have an easy way of getting away from them."

"Air Elemites can *fly?*"

"Yep."

"That's so cool."

"Any more questions?"

"So can Vampires turn into bats?"

"No," he laughed. "That's a myth. They don't sleep in coffins, the sunlight doesn't hurt them and they can cross over water. But, the sunlight and water myths were based on true things. Vampires don't want to be discovered, so they avoid the sunlight because their fangs only come out in sunlight and the sunlight gives them blood red eyes. They can cross water, but they don't like to because, as I said, water makes them weaker. They want to avoid it as much as possible. The myth about a stake to the heart is true, though."

"So if I stab a wooden stake through a Vampire's heart it'll die?"

"Yep."

"Sweet. Anyways, do Elemites have any weaknesses?"

"Yes," he said sadly. "Vampires can rip us apart just as easily as we can rip them apart. But, because we have flesh and blood, it's not necessary for them to rip our heads off if they want to kill us. They just have to make us bleed to death. That is, if they can resist the smell of blood long enough for us to die from that. Vampire venom is one of our other weaknesses. If a Vampire bites you, it's fatal. You'll die in about ten seconds."

"Wait, I thought that if a Vampire bites you then you turn into a Vampire."

"Humans turn into Vampires when Vampires bite them. Elemites die."

"Oh, okay. Keep going."

"Another thing is that we can burn just as easily as humans can, except for Fire Elemites. Water Elemites have the ability to quickly put the fire out, of course. The fact that we have flesh and blood gives us yet another weakness. Animals can break our skin just as easily as they can with a human's. The difference is that Animal Elemites have power over them and other Elemites can easily fight back. And Vampires can't make the animals come attack us. We have only one other weakness and that is that we can drown. The only exception to that rule is Water Elemites. The good thing, though, is that we heal quickly."

"Interesting," I replied. Each time he answered one of my questions, I just thought of more.

Chapter 8

Any More Magical Creatures?

"Did you have any more questions?" Sam asked me.

"You were going to tell me about Unicorns, remember?"

"Oh, right. Unicorns," he started, "look like white horses with a spiraling silver horn on the top of their heads. They hide from humans and their blood is very foul tasting to Vampires. They can run a lot faster than horses—or even Elemites—and their horns can glow in the dark. They can also tell what you're feeling; though they can't tell the reason you are feeling it. Oh yeah, and they can talk, too. Except when they talk, it's more like you're hearing it with your mind than your ears. Kind of like telepathy. Anything else?"

"Are there any more imaginary creatures I should know about?"

"First of all, they're not really imaginary, but I know what you mean. And yes. There are two types: the ones with human-like intelligence that can communicate with humans and the ones with less-than-human intelligence that cannot communicate with humans. Elemites, Vampires, and Unicorns are included in the group with human-like intelligence. The others in that group are Mermaids, Elves, Pixies, and Fairies."

"You're kidding."

"Nope. Which one would you like to hear about first?"

"How about Mermaids?"

"Okay. Mermaids and Mermen can tell whether or not you're an Elemite and they only come out if you are. They also have the ability to know when someone is lying. Those are the only magical powers they have. Otherwise they're just people with tailfins who can breathe underwater. Which one do you want to learn about next?"

"Pixies."

"Pixies have dragonfly wings with little miniature human bodies and people often mistake them for dragonflies. They never fly close enough for a human to realize that they're not actually dragonflies. They can tell if you're an Elemite and they don't have a problem approaching you if you are. They also have the power to predict when a tornado is going to hit. Most of the tornado watchers are Elemites—especially Air Elemites—who have a little Pixie friend helping them. Okay, now which one?"

"Can you list them off again?"

"The ones we haven't done are Elves and Fairies," he told me.

"Okay, Fairies."

"Fairies are kind of like Pixies only with butterfly wings and they glow in the dark, so they stay hidden at night. They can't predict tornadoes, but they can control the temperature. They don't have total control though. There's a one mile distance limit and they can't change the temperature any more than eighty degrees from the natural temperature. They don't really like to, though, because they don't like to disturb any creatures in their natural environments. Plus, if they exert their powers too much for too long, it wears them out quite a bit. Oh and when they get angry, they burst into flames, so be careful."

"You mean they burn up and die?"

"No, of course not! They're immune to fire."

"Oh, okay. I guess that makes more sense. Tell me about Elves now."

"Elves are like Elemites and Vampires in the fact that they can pass for human. That is, if they keep the tips of their ears covered. They also tend to be pretty tall, but not so tall that they get a lot of funny looks from people. They average between six and six and a half feet. The men tend to be closer to six and a half feet and the women tend to be closer to six feet. But remember, that's the average, so there are some that are taller than that."

"Wait," I interrupted. "Aren't Elves like little men that work for Santa and fix shoes and bake cookies in a tree and stuff?"

"No. I don't know where those stories came from, but real Elves are more like the Elves in *The Lord of the Rings*."

"Oh."

"Elves have the ability to see things past, present, and future. To see into the past, they need to be touching a person and then they can see into their past. It also works with objects, but it's a little harder. Seeing into the future is the same concept, only it doesn't work for objects. Seeing into the present is simple. They can see everything that is going on anywhere in the world right now in the present. Another magical ability they have is to heal dying plants and brighten up flowers and things like that. They can't grow plants out of nothing like Earth Elemites can, but their effect on plants is still powerful. Elves are technically immortal because they can't die of old age or get sick, but they can die of all the same injuries that humans can. They are also extremely talented with a bow and arrow and a sword."

"Okay, now what are the other creatures that can't communicate with humans?"

"There are three of them: Giants, Dragons, and Griffins," he said. "Now, because they don't have the same level of intelligence that people do and because they can't communicate with us, you have to remember that they are dangerous. Now, which one would you like to hear about first?"

"How about Giants?"

"Giants generally live in cold places like the tops of tall mountains like the Himalayas or at the North Pole or even in Antarctica. They avoid civilization whenever possible and they are generally very territorial. Giants are no shorter than twelve feet tall when they are full grown, but I've never heard of one taller than fifteen feet. They're pretty much like huge people only they are built a little beefier and they're not as bright."

"Okay, tell me about Dragons, now."

"Dragons like to live in the mountains. Their scales range in color, but they are said to be very shiny and beautiful and harder than steel. They range from 50 to 60 feet long from head to tail and their wingspan is just as long. They can breathe fire and have rows of sharp teeth like a shark. They are very protective of their nests, so if you happen across one of them, there's pretty much no hope for you. They are immune to fire and are generally smarter than Giants, but they lack the ability to form words the way we can. As long as you're not near one of their nests, they usually won't bother you, but try to steer clear of them anyway. Okay, now what do we have left?"

"Griffins, right?"

"Oh yeah. Okay, so Griffins are interesting creatures. They are like a mixture between lions and eagles. They have the back end of a lion and the front half of an eagle. Basically, their body, back legs, and tail are like a lion and their head, front legs, and wings are like an eagle. They are very vicious and protective of their nests like Dragons, but unlike Dragons they will attack you even if you're minding your own business.

You see, to Dragons, humans and Elemites are so small that we are beneath their notice, kind of like insects. But to Griffins, we are the perfect size for prey. They like to live up on cliffs and stuff like eagles, so be on your guard if you happen to be somewhere like that."

I made a mental note to steer clear of cliffs from now on.

Chapter 9

Fatty and Max

"Is that all your questions?" Sam asked me.

"No. When can I meet your family?"

He laughed. "How about tomorrow?"

"Same time?"

"Sure," he answered. "I'll pick you up for school in the morning so I can drive you to my house after school. I'm pretty sure you don't know where my house is. But for today, I have someone else I want you to meet." He gestured over to the edge of the woods and when I looked where he was pointing, I gasped. What I saw were two big grizzly bears coming out of the bushes and walking towards us on all fours. They sat down about five or six yards away from us and stared.

"Christa," he said. "I'd like you to meet my friends Fatty and Max." He gestured to each of the bears in turn. Fatty was somewhat bigger than Max and had a slightly shorter snout and slightly longer fur. When you looked at their eyes, you could tell that Max had a little bit higher level of intelligence. I stared at them for a few moments, paralyzed by fear, before finally answering.

"Th-they're bears?" I asked.

He nodded. "Is there anything wrong?"

I shook my head. "I've just had a bad history with bears."

"I'm sorry. Is it about what happened a few weeks ago? Because that wasn't the same bear. I'm sorry if I upset you."

I shook my head. "No…It's ok…It's just…never mind."

I took a deep breath and told myself that I shouldn't be mad at Fatty and Max for what the other bears did. It didn't matter how much pain those bears caused me over the years, these bears weren't responsible.

Cautiously, I stepped over to Max and touched him lightly on the cheek with a shaking hand, then recoiled. I looked to Sam for support and when he nodded encouragingly, I hesitantly stroked Max's cheek. His fur was both rough and soft at the same time. It reminded me of my dream. The one where I was hugging the bear. Fatty wasn't about to let Max get away with all of the attention. He lumbered over on all fours to nudge me on the side with his nose. I gasped and threw my arms up in the air and froze. Sam came over and stood next to me. "It's okay, he won't hurt you, trust me."

"They're really nice, I guess." I said, a little unsure of myself. I was starting to warm up to them, but only just a little. "I've always wanted a pet, but my mom wouldn't allow it," I added jokingly. He laughed.

There was a short silence as we stared at each other. Then he started slowly leaning towards me until he gently touched his lips to mine. His lips were warm and soft. I reached up and put my hand on his face. Suddenly Max made an irritated noise and we both turned to look at him. He was covering his eyes and had his head turned away from us. We both started laughing.

"Oh yeah, I just remembered. I have one more thing to explain to you."

"Ok, go ahead," I replied.

"Even though Elemites still obey human laws, we also have laws of our own. The Elders of the Ancient Council are the ones that govern the Elemite world. We call them the Elders for short. There are ten Elders, one for every kind of Elemite and one for each of the magical creatures that have human-like intelligence except for Vampires. They don't want a seat on the council and it's probably a good thing, too, because all that Elemite blood in one room might be too tempting for them. The Elders represent their kind and they also use their powers to monitor us to make sure we don't break the rules and to judge us in court to see if we're guilty. The Elf's ability to see the past, present, and future comes in handy and so does the Mermaid's ability to discern between truth and lies and the Unicorn's ability to read emotions. Each Elder is at least 115 years old except for the Unicorn because they don't live that long. The main rule is that you keep the secret, although they do make exceptions sometimes. The other rule is that you don't hunt or kill any other magical creature unless it's in self-defense."

"Okay, so what happens if you break either of the rules?"

"If you tell the secret, you get your symbol confiscated—permanently. You will still have your super human powers, but you won't be able to make the grass grow faster or make a room brighter any more. If you kill another magical creature for any reason other than self-defense or the defense of others," he continued, "you get executed."

"Oh," I said. "I guess that sounds fair."

"I think it's time for us to go," he sighed. "I've got to help Chelsea with her science project."

"Wait, I have one more question." He waited. "When you first started questioning me, on the first day of school, you said that I live with my mom. But you said it as a statement, not a question. I was wondering how you knew that."

He sighed. "When I first met you and saved you from the bear, I knew you were going to be an Elemite. That made me curious and I wanted to know who you were, so I asked if anybody knew you. They told me that you lived with your mom and younger siblings."

"Wait. How did you know that I was going to be an Elemite?"

"Elemites have a slightly different heartbeat than humans, but the difference is so small that human doctors can't hear it. Only Elemites, Mermaids, Pixies, Unicorns, Fairies, Elves, Vampires, Giants, Dragons, Griffins, and certain kinds of animals can," he answered, listing them off on his fingers.

"I have one more question."

"You said that already."

I continued anyways. "How old are you?"

"Just turned eighteen today."

"Oh, happy birthday! Are you really eighteen, or is that just when you stopped aging?"

"No, I'm really eighteen," he laughed. "Elemites aren't immortal. But we don't age normally either. After making the change, our aging process slows to about half of a human's."

"That's kind of weird. So how old is Grandpa George *really*?"

"Grandpa George is really 135 years old." My jaw dropped.

"*135?*"

"Yeah. He's actually our Great Great Great Grandfather. He found out that he had some living descendants that had inherited his Elemite gene rather than his wife's human gene. You see, Grandpa George is a Senior Elemite. Any Elemite over 115 is considered a Senior Elemite. Senior Elemites have powers that are a bit weakened with age. They usually find some Youngling Elemites to help protect them. In return, they teach them about Elemites and how to use their powers. So, Grandpa George adopted us."

"Wow."

"Are you done?"

"Last question, I promise."

"Fine."

"What exactly can an Animal Elemite do?"

"We can control animals and communicate with them over long distances."

"How does the controlling thing work?"

"I thought you were done with the questions."

"Please? I'm curious."

"Fine," he agreed. "We mess with their instincts to make them more likely to do what we want. It doesn't completely take away their free will, though. Animals are perfectly capable of ignoring their instincts. They just don't often do that. Most of them aren't intelligent enough. We can also make ourselves seem more likeable and trustable to them."

"Ok. I'm done with the questioning. Well, I guess I'll see you tomorrow."

"See you tomorrow. I'll be at your house bright and early to pick you up." He smiled. His smile still dazzled me. I had to think for a second before I could answer.

"Right. Bye Fatty! Bye Max!" I waved and to my amazement and amusement, they waved back. Wow. Bears were smarter than I thought.

While I was driving home, I decided that I'd cook dinner for my family for a change instead of just letting my mom do it. Then I realized that I didn't know how to cook. Maybe I could make macaroni and cheese or something. That sounded good. The directions were simple and printed right on the box.

I got dinner ready before my mom got home.

"Oh, thank you, Christa," she said when she came through the kitchen door. "That was so sweet of you to make dinner for us. So what have you been up to today?"

"Nothing much," I answered. "Hey, can I go to Sam Campton's house after school tomorrow?"

"The Campton's? Aren't they that new family?" she asked.

"Yeah."

"Sure Christa, go ahead."

"Thanks Mom."

After dinner I went upstairs and did my homework. When I was done I took a shower and got in bed with a smile on my face. I was really excited about tomorrow.

Chapter 10

The Camptons

Sam picked me up for school the next day, just like he promised. His car was a dirty, faded blue pick-up truck.

"I like your truck."

"Thanks. I bought it myself."

We got in the truck and he started driving down the road.

"Tell me something," he asked me.

"What?"

"Have you ever," he paused and started over. "Have you ever had a boyfriend before?"

"No," I answered, blushing. "Not anyone that you could technically call a 'boyfriend'. I did go out with one guy a couple of times, though."

"And who was that?"

"Colby Markson," I replied. "We only went out a couple of times and I wasn't planning on making him my boyfriend."

"What happened to him?"

"He moved to Wisconsin about a year ago."

"And that's all?" he asked. "You've never had any other relationships?"

"Unless I'm including you, then no. I haven't."

"Interesting."

"What about you?"

"Never."

"Never?"

"No one has ever really appealed to me. And I didn't want to have a girlfriend because I was afraid that my secret would be found out."

"I see."

"Of course, with you, neither of those things are problems," he said, smiling at me.

We arrived at school and Rachel spotted us getting out of his car. Her eyes bugged out and a smile stretched across her face. She nudged Jen who was walking beside her. She turned her head and looked where Rachel was pointing. They wore matching expressions of excitement and burning curiosity.

He walked me to Spanish where I sat down in the empty seat next to Ben.

"So," Ben started, sounding a little nervous and hurt. "I saw you walking with the new kid today. What's his name?" I could hear real disappointment in his voice.

"Sam," I told him.

"Right, him." This time he sounded more annoyed than disappointed. It sounded like he didn't care what his name was. He probably didn't even care that he *had* a name. He just asked to be polite. "So are you like dating him or something?"

"I guess you could say that."

"Oh." He looked down at his hands. "Well then, I guess I'm happy for you." I sighed. This wasn't going to get any easier.

The rest of the morning passed pretty much like that with Jenny asking pretty much the same basic questions that Ben had except that she seemed mildly excited about it. She was happy for me. In History, Sam asked me if I was ready to go meet his family.

"I'm just a little nervous," I answered. "What if I trip and fall and make a fool of myself?"

"Don't worry," he reassured me. "You get more graceful as your powers come in."

"Are you sure?"

"I'm sure." I hoped he was. I didn't want to be the world's first and only clumsy Elemite.

I brought Sam to sit with us at lunch which brought on an onslaught of questions in my fourth and sixth period classes from Rachel and Matt, but mostly Rachel. Chelsea was excited that I was coming over after school and chattered with me all through Art. I was getting both more excited and more nervous by the second.

Finally, I was riding in Sam's truck as he drove towards his house.

"I have a late birthday present for you," I told him.

"That's really nice of you, Christa. You didn't have to get me anything." I reached into my backpack and pulled out the painting I made of him in Art. He pulled into his driveway and put the truck in park. I handed him the painting.

"This is really great, Christa!" he exclaimed. "You made this yourself?"

"Yep."

"Wow, you're really talented. Thanks."

We got out of the car and he held my hand before I turned to look at the house. It was two stories, painted a bright and cheery yellow. It had a big white porch in the front and colorful flowers in every window. It was beautiful. I noticed several cars sitting out front.

"Whose cars are those?" I asked.

"The black one is Brian's, the blue bug is Chelsea's, and the green one is Tasha and Kyle's."

He led me into the house where his family was waiting. A woman with wavy brown hair and blue eyes came up to me.

"Hi, I'm Tasha," she said, shaking my hand. "But you probably already guessed that." She smiled. Her words and her smile were so kind and reassuring that my nervousness completely vanished. Chelsea bounced over to my side, a huge smile on her face.

"It's nice to see you again," she said as she hugged me.

I laughed. "You just saw me in Art today," I pointed out. "That was only two classes ago."

"I know. But that's a long time in my opinion." I laughed and everybody joined in.

"I'm Brian." He was the same boy who was sitting with Sam a few days ago.

"Yeah, I saw you sitting with Sam the other day, so I assumed that's who you were."

"I'm Kyle," a second man said, shaking my hand. Kyle was muscular, but thin. He had blond hair and hazel eyes.

"And this is Grandpa George," Sam announced, leading a kind looking old man towards me. His hand felt old and leathery, but also soft and gentle when I shook it. He had a sweet smile with salt and pepper colored hair. He was about the same height as Sam and was using a cane to help support himself.

"It's a pleasure to meet you, dear," he said kindly.

"It's so nice to meet all of you," I told them. "Your home is really very beautiful." The inside walls of the house were white with hard wood floors. There was a black sofa and recliner facing towards a flat screen TV. There was a lamp in the corner and a staircase to the left of the front room we were in. An opening in the far right corner led to the dining room and kitchen area and a hallway near the stairs led to some other part of the house.

"Come on," Sam said. "I'll show you the rest of the house." He took my hand and led me down the hallway. There were two doors in the hallway.

"The one on the right is Grandpa George's room and the one on the left is his study."

"Would you like to see some of my old photographs?" said a voice from behind us. We turned around to see Grandpa George standing in the hallway behind us.

"I'd love to see some of your old photographs," I answered. We followed him into his study. Shelves of books lined the walls. So many that it could rival the local library in town. He walked over to his desk and opened a drawer. He reached in and lifted out an old photo album.

"Here we are," he said. Sam and I walked over to the desk and pulled up a couple of chairs to sit in. Grandpa George opened up the album and pointed to the first picture. "This was in 1932. It was our first family photo that included our grandchildren. That's my wife, Martha. She would have been about forty-four in that picture. I would have been about thirty-seven or thirty-eight physically which means that I was really about fifty-eight. There's my son and his wife. My son was an Air Elemite and his wife was human. She died of old age and my son was killed in a Vampire attack. The boy sitting on my lap is my grandson, Mark. That would make him Tasha, Sam, and Brian's great grandfather. He was human like his grandmother and mother before him. He was four years old in that picture."

"Where is he now?"

"He died of a heart attack six years ago when he was seventy-five."

"I'm sorry," I said. "It must be hard to outlive your grandchildren."

"It's ok, Christa. He lived a good long life."

"I got to meet him once," Sam said. "It was when I was eleven and a half, so it was just after Grandpa George adopted us and just before he died. It was strange because he looked the same age as Grandpa George, but I knew he was his grandson."

We turned the page to look at the rest of the photo album. He had pictures that dated back to the Great Depression and Pearl Harbor. It was fun to turn the pages and watch each decade of the 1900's go by. The last picture in the photo album looked like a fairly recent one of all of them together standing in front of the Statue of Liberty.

"This picture was taken about six months ago. Not too long before we moved here," Grandpa George explained. He closed the photo album and put it away. "Well, I best be going," he said. Sam and I stood up to leave.

"Thanks for letting us look at your photo album Mr. Robertson," I said.

"Please, call me Grandpa George." Sam led me out the door and back into the hallway. We rounded the corner and I followed him up the stairs.

"This is Chelsea's room…Brian's room…Tasha and Kyle's room…and this is my room," he said gesturing to the doors. We stopped when we reached his room. He looked down at me and opened the door. He had a double bed in the far right corner with a white comforter and dark blue pillow cases. There was a window on the right hand wall just over his bed. His floor was a soft, cream colored carpet. His white walls were lined with shelves of CDs, books, and movies. The TV was to the right of the door and on the same wall as it. It had a twenty-two inch screen and a DVD player on the shelf beneath it. There was a desk with a computer and a family picture on the right wall. I noticed that the family picture wasn't recent. It didn't even have the same people as the one in the back of the photo album. I walked over to the desk and picked up the picture.

The woman looked a lot like Tasha, but she was older and had green eyes. The man didn't look anything like Kyle, but he looked kind of like Brian. The only differences were that he had slightly shorter hair and a different nose. Brian's nose looked a lot like the woman's. The girl looked like a younger version of Tasha. Or a younger version of the woman. It depends on how you look at it. She looked like she was about thirteen or fourteen. The older boy looked like a perfect mix between the man and woman and appeared to be about nine or ten. I looked closer and realized he looked like a younger Sam. The younger boy looked about a year younger than the older boy and looked like a younger version of the man. Or a younger Brian. I assumed that this was a picture of Tasha, Sam, and Brian with their parents before they died. Sam walked over to stand by me.

"That was our last family picture before my parents died," he said quietly. So I was right about who the people in the picture were.

"Do you miss them?" What a stupid question. Of course he did.

"Very much," he answered softly. His voice was saturated with pain. He probably felt the same way about his parents as I felt about my dad. I turned and wrapped my arms around his waist. He put his arms around me and rested his chin on the top of my head. I pulled away slightly and stretched up on my toes to press my lips lightly to his. He pulled away after a couple of seconds and smiled at me.

"Now that you've met my family," he said. "It's my turn to meet yours."

Chapter 11

Warm Welcome

"Hey Mom," I called when I walked in the door, "Can I bring someone over tomorrow to meet you?" She was sitting on the couch watching her favorite soap opera.

"Sure honey. Is it that Sam guy you were hanging out with today?"

"Yep, that's him."

"Ok. When do you want him to come over?"

"How about at six so he can stay for dinner?"

"That'll be great, Christa. I'm looking forward to meeting your new boyfriend." She looked over the back of the couch and grinned at me.

"Ah Mom!" I whined. "*Please* don't embarrass me! I'm begging you."

"Ok, ok, I'll be good, I promise." She smiled.

"Thanks Mom." I called Sam and told him when to come before skipping upstairs to my room. I turned to my dresser and pulled out an old pair of sweats and a baggy t-shirt to change into for bed. Then I crossed the hall to the bathroom to brush my teeth. I went back to my room and turned to my bookshelf which held my books, my drawing pads, and my CD's. I plucked my favorite book off the shelf and plopped down on my bed to read it, hoping that it would make the time pass quicker. It worked like a charm. Before I knew it, I was fast asleep.

I had the same dream as I had had the night before school started. Only this time, I knew what it meant. *I was floating,*

floating out in the open ocean with thousands of tiny fish surrounding me. Then the scene changed and I was in the forest and I was hugging a big black bear. I only recognized that part of the woods because I had had this dream before. Otherwise, the place was completely unfamiliar. Then I was lying out on the grass in a big field, letting the sun warm my skin. Suddenly I was flying. I was soaring with the birds, twirling and whirling through the clouds, more free than I've ever felt before. The picture changed and I was suddenly planting some seeds. After they were planted, I stepped back and watched as they suddenly grew into three giant sunflowers. Then I let myself fall backwards until I landed on something soft. I opened my eyes and was back in my room.

I rolled over in my bed and looked at the clock on my nightstand. It was seven in the morning. Might as well get up and take a shower. I went to my dresser and picked out a nice pair of jeans and a white button-up blouse. I walked down the hall and got a towel out of the cupboard before carrying it all into the bathroom.

After I took a shower, I went downstairs to get myself a bowl of cereal. I ate my cereal in silence, trying to get the time to pass more quickly. I finished my cereal and got up to rinse it in the sink. Then I had a sudden inspiration. Instead of turning the handle to get the water flowing out of the faucet, I concentrated with my mind. The faucet turned on, just like I wanted. I smiled to myself and rinsed out my bowl.

I went back upstairs to my room and looked at my cell phone that was sitting on my dresser. I had a text from Rachel.

Hey!

I hit the 'reply' button and typed her back an answer.

Hey! Wats up?

Do u want 2 go 2 a movie w/ me 2nite?

Sry. I cant. I got plans.

Oh. Do the plans have 2 do w/ Sam?

U guessed it. ☺

K. But u got 2 tell me about it monday.

K in study hall. He will b sitting w/ us at lunch.

Sounds good. G2G. Bye!

Bye!

I put my phone back on my dresser and scooped my favorite book up off the floor where it had fallen sometime the night before. I set it on my bedside table. I needed something to help pass the time, so I decided to do laundry. I picked some dirty clothes up off the floor and threw them in my hamper. Then I lifted my full hamper up into my arms and started heading towards the laundry room.

"Oh, hey Tracy," I greeted her when she came into the hallway. She answered me with a yawn. I could tell by her face that she had just woken up and was still not fully awake. She was probably on her way to breakfast. "I was just going to do a load of laundry. Do you have anything you want me to throw in the wash for you?"

"Yeah," she answered groggily. "Could you wash my red blouse? It's on the end of my bed."

"Sure thing, Trace." She yawned and I headed into her room to grab the blouse off the end of her bed before heading downstairs to the washing machine.

I threw a load in the wash and then walked back up the stairs to do my homework. When the load was done, I put it in the dryer and stuck another load in the wash. I kept it up until my homework and the laundry were finished. Afterwards, I went back upstairs to give Tracy her shirt back.

Laundry and homework did exactly what I wanted them to: they killed time and got something accomplished. I didn't know what to do next, so I decided to go get some lunch. I started work today and my shift started at noon, so I might as well get lunch now.

After lunch I went upstairs and grabbed my purse and cell phone so I could go to work. I ran back down stairs to find my mom.

"Hey Mom," I said when I found her in the living room. "I'm on my way to work."

"Ok sweetie, have a good day." I walked out the door and down the driveway to my car. It was a nice sunny day outside and I was loving it. The sunlight coming in through my window felt good on my skin.

I drove through town until I arrived at Carson's Convenience Store. I parked in the employee parking area and then went around to the front and walked in.

"Hello Christa! How are you today?" Mike Carson greeted me cheerily.

"Hello Mr. Carson. I'm fine. How are you?"

"I'm fine, thank you. Are you ready for work?"

"Yes sir. What do you want me to do?"

"Well, I figure since it's your first day, you can start by restocking the shelves. Here are the boxes of merchandise. All you have to do is put it on the shelves. Kenton will help you if you have any questions."

Work was calming and I found that I enjoyed it even more than I thought I would. I restocked the shelves, helped a few customers and watched as Kenton showed me how to work the register.

When I got home, I didn't have anything to do, so I went upstairs, grabbed my drawing pad and started drawing. When I was finished, it was a very detailed picture of Sam with Fatty and Max. I looked at the clock. Finally, it was time to start preparing dinner. I skipped down to the kitchen to help my mom.

I was glad that I wasn't a good cook because then it took that much more of my concentration to help my mom, which made it a lot easier to keep my mind off waiting. I did manage to give myself a small cut on my finger, but when I turned my hand over to look at it, it was already a scab. Sam really wasn't kidding about Elemites healing quickly.

And then there was a knock on the door. I followed my mom out of the kitchen and down the hallway to the door. She turned the knob and there he was, looking gorgeous as always.

"You must be Sam," she greeted him. "It's so nice to meet you. Come on in."

"Thank you Mrs. McCalliston," he replied.

"You can call me Linda." I couldn't help beaming at them. So far, so good.

"Christa, why don't you show Sam to the kitchen and set the table," my mom continued. "I'll go get Tracy and Collin." I nodded at her and took Sam's hand, leading him to the kitchen.

"You can go ahead and have a seat at the table if you want," I said, turning to the cupboard to retrieve some plates. He didn't listen to me. Instead, he came up behind me and started getting the cups.

"So what do you think so far?" I asked him.

"You have a very nice home and your mom is very hospitable," he replied.

"Thank you," my mom said as she walked through the door into the kitchen. Sam and I smiled at each other. Tracy wasn't too far behind my mom, but when she got to the doorway, she stopped.

"What is it?" Collin asked from behind her, craning his neck to see into the kitchen.

"That's Sam?" she asked me incredulously, her eyes wide. I nodded. Her lips stretched up into a smile. "Hi Sam," she said, waving her fingers at him. I rolled my eyes. We all sat at the table and dinner was served.

Sam was bombarded with questions all through dinner. I couldn't figure out how he could possibly eat when he constantly had to answer questions, but he managed.

After dinner we went into the living room to socialize. After a while, Collin had a project to work on, Tracy went up to her room to do whatever it was she wanted to do and Mom went to go do the dishes. And that meant that finally, we were left alone.

"Ah," I sighed, leaning into him, wrapping my arms around his waist, and resting my head on his chest. "Alone at last." He wrapped his arms around me and rested his cheek on the top of my head. We sat there for a moment and then he lifted his head and pulled away slightly so he could look at me.

"I was thinking," he started. I looked up at him, waiting. "It's your birthday on Saturday, right?"

"Yes."

"So, I was thinking that maybe we could go to Portland for the day and we could see a movie and get some dinner and just spend time together."

"Like a date?" I asked. "Like our first official date?"

"Sure."

I smiled. "Ok." I rested my head on his chest again and he rested his cheek on my hair like before. We sat like that for a moment and this time it was me who broke the silence.

"Let's meet in the meadow tomorrow. And bring Fatty and Max."

"Ok." We sat there for a moment and then he sighed. I looked up at him.

"I should get going," he explained.

"Ok," I said, sitting up.

"I'll see you tomorrow." He kissed me on the top of the head and then he was gone.

Chapter 12

Dad

I woke up the next day and got dressed in my old blue jeans and a green t-shirt. I poured myself a bowl of cereal and sat down to eat it. I ate all the cereal and then drank the milk straight from the bowl. I put my bowl in the sink and then went upstairs to brush my hair. After I got all of the snarls out of it, I brushed my teeth thoroughly before skipping down the stairs and out the front door.

I walked down the driveway to my car with a smile on my face. It was sunny and it felt good. I backed out of the driveway and headed into the woods. The memories of my dad slowly got rid of my good mood and I was soon watery eyed, but I made sure I got rid of it quickly before Sam could see that I had been crying.

I got out of the car and hiked over the small hill into the clearing. Sam was waiting and he had Fatty and Max, just like I had asked him. He was sitting on the ground between them, scratching behind Fatty's ears. Max's head rested in his lap. I was still getting used to seeing bears act so friendly towards humans. Well, I guess we weren't really human, but we *looked* human. I may have warmed up to the bears a bit, but they still made me a bit uneasy.

Sam looked up and smiled when he heard me approach.

"Hey, Christa!" he called waving at me. I smiled and waved back, walking towards him. I arrived at the spot where he sat and plopped down on the ground on the other side of Max.

"And how are you today?" he asked.

"I'm good. You?"

"I'm good. So why did you want to come here today?"

"I just wanted to spend time with you, Fatty, and Max. Get some fresh air, enjoy the day, hang out, spend time with you."

"It is a very nice day."

Neither one of us spoke for a few moments which gave my mind time to wander. Giving my mind time to wander wasn't such a good idea when I was in the clearing and I had to hold back my tears. I glanced over at Sam and noticed that he was watching me. He had a concerned expression on his face. I tried to smile at him, but I had a feeling it was pretty unconvincing.

"I noticed that you look a little bit…sad every time you come here," he said softly. "And I was wondering why that was." I hesitated and looked at my hands. "You don't have to tell me if you don't want to."

"No it's fine," I told him. "It's my dad."

"Your dad?" he asked confused, curious, and concerned all at once.

"Yeah," I answered. "My dad and I would go on walks down here all the time. Sometimes he would come here by himself so he could have alone time." I hesitated before continuing. "He died here. He was alone and there was a bear…" I could feel the lump in my throat and the tears in my eyes. I tried to choke them back. "They found his body a day later. There were bear tracks all over the place. I was only eleven years old when it happened. I remember being in shock, not believing it at first. I remember thinking that he couldn't be dead. It just wasn't possible. I miss him so much."

I could feel the tears streaming freely now. Sam's arms wrapped around me and I leaned into him, resting my head on his shoulder. We just sat there for a while and I let him gently rock me until I stopped crying.

"I'm sorry," I apologized to him as I started sitting up and wiping the tears from my eyes with the back of my hand. "You don't have to sit here while I cry. It's not fair to you."

"It's completely fine. I don't mind," he responded.

"Sorry I ruined your shirt."

"It's ok," he answered, looking down at his shirt. "This one's old and I got plenty of other ones. Besides, it's just tears." We sat there like that for a few more moments with me leaning into him, comforted by his strong arms around me. Finally I broke the silence.

"The real reason I wanted to come out here with you is to relax and kind of get away from it all," I told him. "I have a lot going on in my life right now. I mean, my senior year just started and I have a lot of homework and stuff, but I also just found out that I'm an Elemite. And on top of all that, this time of year always reminds me of my dad because the anniversary of his death is coming up in a few weeks. I just got a lot on my plate."

"I can see what you mean." There was silence for a few more moments before I broke it again.

"You know what?" I asked.

"What?"

"I think that I should start training. I want to learn everything I can so I won't be defenseless in a Vampire attack. You can teach me more about how to be an Animal Elemite and Grandpa George and Tasha can teach me how to be an Earth Elemite. Then there's Chelsea and Brian who can teach me how to be a Water and Air Elemite. And Kyle can teach me how to be a Fire Elemite."

"That sounds reasonable. How about starting tomorrow?"

"Sounds great! And can we start with you teaching me how to be an Animal Elemite?"

"Ok," he answered. "Meet me here tomorrow and we'll get started."

"Sounds good." I got up and started walking to my car. I looked over my shoulder as I walked away and smiled. "See you tomorrow." He smiled and waved as I continued walking up the hill and out of the clearing.

Back at home I decided to practice using my powers on my own, just to get a glimpse of what I could do. I practiced flipping the lights in my room on and off. It took a little effort after a while, so I stopped.

I went down stairs and practiced using my powers to turn on the faucet in the kitchen. When the water starting flowing I practiced turning it off again. Bored of the faucet, I looked around the kitchen for something else to practice on. The flower in the window caught my eye and I walked over to examine it. It looked a little droopy, so I concentrated on making it better. The stem immediately straightened out and the petals brightened. I smiled and went back upstairs to my room.

I tried to see if I could tidy up my desk a little by blowing some of the papers into a pile. The breeze was a little stronger than I had intended and papers blew all over my room.

"Oops," I whispered as I bent over to pick up my room. "Maybe I should just lay off on using my powers until training."

Chapter 13

Training

The next morning was Labor Day which meant no school, so after lunch I drove to the normal spot in the woods. It still bothered me, but I was more able to handle it now.

"What's first?" I asked Sam when I arrived in the clearing. I was kind of nervous about training, but my excitement outweighed it by quite a bit.

"Establishing trust," Sam answered.

"Ok. How do I do that?"

"You send a feeling of trust through your mind to the animal. Let's start with an easy one," he said. "Like a rabbit. They tend be a bit more trusting than most animals." Just then a cute little grey bunny rabbit hopped towards us out of the forest.

"Oh how cute!"

"So just send a message of trust and then he'll let you pet him." I nodded and concentrated on getting the bunny to trust me.

"Come on little guy. I won't hurt you," I told the bunny in my mind. It cautiously hopped towards me once and stopped. *"It's ok. You got nothing to worry about,"* I reassured him. I was trying not to let the bunny sense my nervousness. I knelt down and stretched out my hand as he hopped over and sniffed my fingers. I stretched my hand further and pet it on the head. *"You can trust me."* The bunny hopped into my lap and I held it in my arms. I was still pretty nervous, but petting the bunny made me feel better.

"Well done," Sam congratulated me.

"What's next?" I asked.

"Now we try an animal that doesn't trust as easily."

"Ok. What cute little animal do I get to pet next?"

"A raccoon."

"A raccoon?"

"Yes. A raccoon."

I put the bunny down and watched it hop into the bushes at the edge of the line of trees. I didn't like the sound of a raccoon. Raccoons were mean, so if I messed up, the results might not be pretty. I tried to calm my nerves as a raccoon walked lazily out of the trees to the left.

"Hey little buddy," I reached out to the raccoon with my mind, willing him to trust me. *"I'm not going to hurt you. It's okay."*

The raccoon took a few wary steps towards me and stopped, looking anxious. He sniffed the air and took another step towards me.

"It's alright. I'm an Animal Elemite. It's fine."

The raccoon crept cautiously over to me, sniffed, and let me pat his head. It was a weird experience, petting a raccoon. Not many people get to do that.

"Congrats, Christa. You just passed your first lesson in Animal Elemite training."

"Cool. Are there any more fuzzy little animals I get to pet?"

"Next you're going to communicate with the animals," he answered. "So not only will you be able to send messages of trust, you'll send other messages and you'll be able to receive messages."

"Awesome. So it's kind of like talking to animals?"

"Yeah, pretty much. Only, it's in your mind, not out loud. I thought I'd start you off with Fatty and Max since you already know them."

"Sounds good. What do I do?"

"You know when you were sending trust messages?"

"Yeah?"

"Just do that only send whatever message you want."

"Oh," I said simply. It sounded easy enough.

"Hey, Fatty!" I felt a little stupid, but I did it anyways. *"You hungry? I think I saw some berries on a bush over by that tree."*

"Really?" he responded. *"I like berries...Berries are yummy...I want some berries..."* He lumbered off towards the bush by the mentioned tree to check it out.

"What'd you tell him?" Sam asked.

"I told him there were some berries in that bush over there."

"Sweet, he'll enjoy that." He smiled. "Anyways, we have one more lesson. "Healing animals."

"Sounds difficult."

"It is," he answered frankly. He ran off into the forest and came back with a bird that had a broken wing and a squirrel with a bandaged leg. "I found this little guy this morning," he said gesturing to the bird. "And this little fellow not long before you got here."

"Which one am I healing?" It was humbling to be trusted with the responsibility of healing an injured animal. But knowing that I had the ability to heal made me feel responsible for helping whenever I could.

"Broken bones are harder, so I'll do the bird." He handed me the squirrel as he finished speaking. "All you have to do is place your hand over the injury and concentrate really hard." I watched as the bird's wing healed and it suddenly took flight. I looked at the squirrel and took a deep breath. I placed my hand over the bandage and concentrated. I felt my hand getting warmer and it started to tingle a little. I wondered if that was a good sign or a bad sign.

"Take the bandage off now, Christa," he said after a moment or two. I carefully unwrapped the blood-stained bandage.

"I did it," I whispered.

"Well done. Um, everything else to do with Animal Elemites just builds off of those lessons, so just experiment with your powers and it'll be easy to find your full potential. Good work."

"Oh no, work! What time is it?"

He checked his watch. "4:00."

"I got to go. I have to run home and grab something to eat so I can be at work at five."

"Ok. See you later then." He kissed me on the forehead before I hurried off to my car. I began to run and suddenly I was going as fast as a car on the highway. I skidded to a stop and nearly fell over just before smacking into the door of my car.

"What was that?" I asked a little shaken.

"You got your super speed."

"Oh, right, I forgot Elemites had super speed." I opened the door mechanically. "See ya later." I got in the car stiffly and drove to work with thoughts flying around in my head. I was going to have to test out my speed, strength, smell, eyesight, and hearing sometime. This was going to be fun. I knew Elemites had super speed, but I didn't imagine being able to go so fast. I was so focused on my Elemental powers that I totally forgot about the super-human half of my powers.

I pulled into my driveway and walked up the porch steps to the front door. I went inside and looked in the fridge for something to eat. There was leftover hamburger soup. I heated it up in the microwave before sitting down and stirring it with my spoon, watching the meat, carrots, potatoes, beans, and corn travel in circles around the bowl. I thought about my powers and ways to test them as I ate my soup in silence.

I got to work five minutes before five. The automatic doors slid open and I greeted Kenton and Matt as I walked through them, slipping on my blue employee vest.

I busied myself with stacking things on the shelves as I thought about ways to test my powers. When I was done stacking, I slipped into the backroom and found a box that I knew my old self wouldn't have been able to carry. I lifted it easily over my head with one hand and walked around the room, smiling. Putting the box down, I decided to test my hearing by listening out to the parking lot. A car pulled up and two people got out. One of them was a little girl who wanted potato chips.

I closed my eyes and tried to test my sense of smell. The box to my left contained candy bars and the box to my right had apples in it. I opened my eyes and, sure enough, that's exactly how the boxes were labeled. I picked up the box of apples and took it out into the main part of the store and started restocking the apple crate in the fruit section.

The next morning I woke up to my alarm clock. I hit the snooze button, rolled over, and pulled the pillow over my head to block out the light coming in through the window. I didn't want to get up for school. Using my powers as much as I had the day before exhausted me. I was laying on my side holding the pillow over my head like that for a minute or two before I finally decided to get up. I rolled out of bed and got dressed. I began to brush my hair, but I gave up and decided to just put it in a ponytail.

"Buenos días, Christa," Señor Gonzales greeted me as I came in to class.

"Buenos días, Señor Gonzales." I sat down in my usual seat next to Ben and got out my Spanish homework.

"Hey Christa!" Ben beamed at me as I sat down. "How was your weekend?"

"Great," I yawned. "How was yours?"

"It was fine," he answered. "Hey, are you okay, Christa? You sound kind of tired."

"Yeah I'm fine. I just stayed up a little too late last night, that's all." Boy, I'd have to start exercising my powers more often so they wouldn't be so exhausting.

At lunch my friends and I sat out in the courtyard. A bird flew over and I started feeding it bread crumbs from my sandwich.

"That's so cool," Rachel whispered. "It's eating it right out your hand. How do you do that?"

"I'm just lucky, I suppose." The sun started to move behind some clouds and it started getting chilly. I wondered if I could use my powers to keep warm and I slowly started to warm up.

"It's getting cold out here," Rachel complained.

"Don't worry," Matt told her. "I'll keep you warm." He put one of his arms around her and began to rub her arm with his hand. Rachel beamed at me so hugely that I was surprised it fit on her face.

"Aren't you cold, Christa?" Jen asked.

"No, I'm fine."

"You sure?" Rachel asked touching my arm. "Wow, you are warm," she said suddenly. "It's like you're your own space heater."

"That can't be good," Ben commented. "Do you have a fever?"

"No, I'm fine," I assured them. I leaned into Sam and he put his arm around me. I wrapped my arm around his waist in an attempt to keep him warm, too. My powers got better and better all the time.

After school I dropped Tracy and Collin off at home before driving over to Sam's house.

"Hi Christa!" Tasha greeted me with a hug as I came in the door. "You ready?"

"Of course!" I replied. "I can't wait."

"Come with us to the backyard," she instructed. I followed her and Grandpa George out the backdoor and onto the grass. Sam, Brian, Chelsea, and Kyle filed out behind us to watch.

"Now," said Grandpa George. "Grow an apple on this tree."

"What's the point of that?" I asked. "There are already apples on that tree."

"The point is, it exercises your powers," he answered. "And in order to develop your powers you have to start small and work your way up. Growing an apple on this tree is a pretty easy task to do for an Earth Elemite. All you have to do is hold your hand under the branch, concentrate and…" I watched as an apple suddenly grew on the branch until it turned ripe and fell lightly into his outstretched hand. He handed it to me and smiled.

"Now you try," he said. I nodded and stepped up to the tree. I stretched out my hand and concentrated hard. My hand started to tingle as if there was some kind of energy coming out of it that was reaching up to coax the apple to grow. I watched as a tiny apple sprouted on the branch and grew until finally it ripened and fell off the branch, landing gently in my hand. It was an amazing thing to watch.

"What's next?" I asked with a smile, unable to hide my pleasure that I succeeded.

"Let's see if you can grow a green apple even though it's a red apple tree."

I nodded and turned back to the tree. I tried hard, but my apple came out partially red and partially green. I frowned at it, frustrated.

"That's okay," Tasha encouraged. "Try again." I tried as hard as I could and managed to make the next apple come out right. I smiled, proud of myself.

"What do I need to do now?"

"See that tree over there?" Grandpa George asked. He was pointing to a fruitless tree at the other end of the yard. I nodded and he continued. "It's an orange tree and I want you to grow an orange."

"But oranges aren't in season," I reminded him.

"I know," was his simple answer. Instead of arguing, I walked over to the tree and held out my hand. I focused as hard as I could, but nothing happened. I sighed angrily.

"Just keep trying, Christa," Sam said. "I believe in you."

I nodded to him and tried again. This time I managed to produce a tiny baby orange, but that's all. I furrowed my brow in consternation. I tried a third time and to my excitement an orange sprouted on the branch, grew to full size, and dropped into my palm. I turned to Grandpa George and beamed at him.

"Now let's try growing an apple on that orange tree," he told me. I hesitated. I'd had a hard enough time with the orange. Finally I stuck out my hand and gave it a try. To my utter amazement, a shiny red apple came out on the first try.

"Cool," Brian said as he took the apple from my hand and took a bite. Suddenly he got a strange look on his face. "This apple tastes like an orange."

We all laughed and then I sighed and turned to Grandpa George. "I guess that one doesn't count, does it?" He shook his head. I turned back to the tree. Another apple was produced and I took a big bite of it.

"Yep. This one's definitely an apple," I said. Sam smiled at me.

"Ok, let's see how well you do at reviving plants," Tasha told me. She walked over to the garden and showed me a half withered rosebush. “I’ve been purposefully letting this die so I could save it for you,” she said with a smile.

“That was…nice of you.”

“And this one is the one I’m using to show you how to do it.” She turned to a second bush next to the first one and waved her hand over it. The roses brightened and their stems straightened. I tried it on my bush and it worked, but not as well as Tasha’s.

“That’s ok, kiddo. Try again.” I did and they were the most beautiful roses I’d ever seen. Sam walked over, picked one the roses and handed it to me. I blushed.

“We just have three more lessons,” Tasha informed me.

“Can we take a break for a little bit?” I asked. “I’m exhausted.” I sat down on the back patio, leaning against Sam’s shoulder and twirling the rose in my hand. It felt like a bunch of energy had just been drained out of me.

“Sure thing, kiddo.” I smiled at her. Apparently I had a new nickname. Chelsea came out with a glass of water for me and I gladly drank.

“Ok, I think I’m ready.” I got up and handed Sam the rose for safe keeping. “What’s next?”

“Now it’s time to grow something from scratch,” Grandpa George answered. “Let’s grow a sunflower.” He slowly made his way to the edge of the garden. Once there, he waved his hand over the soil and a tiny stem sprouted. He then began to pull his hand upwards as if pulling an invisible piece of string attached to the stem. The stalk grew and bloomed into a sunflower as he pulled its invisible string. As it grew higher than his head, he began making a motion with his hand as if pushing it up. He turned to me, expectant. I nodded and turned to the empty patch of soil in front of me.

I smiled when the stem peeked out from under the soil. I pulled my hand upwards, willing it to grow. Inch by inch it crept higher, reaching for the sky. The flower opened up revealing cheery yellow petals. I pushed upwards, helping it reach its full potential. I finished and smiled at my work. The sunflower was so perfect and bright faced that it appeared to smile right back at me.

"Good!" Tasha exclaimed. "Now it's time for earth moving."

"Earth moving?" It sounded difficult.

"Yeah, it'll be fun." She grabbed my hand and towed me to the middle of the yard. She stomped and the earth shook slightly beneath us.

"That's your first lesson in earth moving," she said. "Quakes." I stomped my foot as hard as I could, but nothing happened.

"That's okay," she reassured me. "Just do it with a little more feeling next time, kiddo."

I stomped my foot harder and willed the quake to happen as hard as I could. This time I felt something. It was like I was sending vibrations from my body down into the ground. The earth shook beneath us so hard that we all tumbled to the ground.

"That was a little strong, but good," Tasha complimented me. "Didn't know you had it in you." We smiled at each other.

"Let's go out in the woods where there's no one around to hurt for this next part," Grandpa George said. "Sorry Sam, Brian, and Chelsea. Only Tasha, Christa, and I get to go." Sam walked up and took my hand.

"Listen to them and be a good girl," he said teasingly. "Be careful," he added more seriously as he walked toward the house.

"Ok, next up, moving rocks," Tasha announced when we arrived in the clearing. "Just hold your hand out palm down. Now close your fingers part-way as if you're holding a baseball. Next you concentrate and pull up and flip your hand over at the same time." I copied her movements and watched as a small rock broke free from the earth and flew up to the level of her hand. I tried a few more times and finally got it to work.

"I did it!"

"That's it! After you get it to that point, you can do whatever you want with it." She made a throwing motion with her hand and the rock shot over the trees on the other side of the clearing.

I hurled the rock as hard as I could and it flew into the air following after Tasha's.

"That was great!" Tasha praised me. "Now try a bigger one." She used both hands this time and lifted a pretty sizeable chunk of earth into the air. But instead of throwing it, she just let it fall back into its place, making the ground shake a little.

"Like this?" I asked. I took a deep breath and broke a piece of earth out of the ground that was two feet in diameter. I was straining from the effort so I just let it fall back in its place just like Tasha did. Then I bent over and put my hands on my knees for support as I panted. All I wanted to do was go home and sleep.

"That was really good. You feeling all right?"

"Yeah, I'm fine."

"Well it's getting late. You should get home. I'll see you tomorrow." She gave me a hug and ran off.

Chapter 14

Fire and Ice

I woke up on Wednesday morning feeling extremely exhausted. I could tell it was going to be a long day.

I rolled out of bed and got ready for the day. My eyes were half shut as I brushed my teeth and hair and trudged down the stairs for breakfast.

I got the cereal and milk out and poured myself a bowl. Just as I finished putting away the box and carton, Collin spoke up.

"Hey can you pour me some too, please?" he asked.

"Ugh," I complained just as Tracy walked in.

"Morning sunshine," she said sarcastically. "Who put grumpy nuts in your cereal?" I glared at her and grumbled as I got up to get Collin some cereal.

In Spanish, Ben was his perky self, but he could tell I was tired, so he cut down on the chit chat a little.

English was fine because Jenny is the type of friend you can be quiet with. It was good for me to have at least one friend like that.

In History, Sam understood exactly why I was tired, so he left me alone.

Then it was lunch time. Everyone came and sat at our table. I wasn't really hungry, so I just leaned against Sam and took a nap. The next thing I knew Sam was nudging me and telling me that it was time for fourth period.

In Study Hall, Rachel could tell I was tired, so she let me take another nap during that hour instead of talking to me the whole time. I felt so much better after that.

Art was nice because I was really rested and could just let my mind explore and be creative, let my hand be free to spoil the clean white easel with the paint in any way it wanted to. I didn't have to work too hard and it was relaxing to mix colors and make abstract shapes appear where before, there was nothing.

And then there was Physics. I'd been dreading it all day. I was already bad at it and today I wasn't as awake as I normally am. I walked into class and trudged to my seat, determined to focus the best I could.

"OK, class, I'm sure you all know that our quiz is tomorrow," Mr. Dexter started.

I didn't know that, I thought. *Maybe I should pay more attention.*

"So today," he continued. "We are going to spend the whole day reviewing."

I couldn't believe it. It was a miracle sent from heaven. I wouldn't have to work so hard after all. *And* I'd be much better prepared for that quiz tomorrow.

After class, I went home in a much better mood. I grabbed a snack and went to meet Sam, Kyle, and Chelsea.

This time, we went down to a secluded spot on Sandy River rather than in the clearing. We decided it was better if I *didn't* start a forest fire and also to have water for Chelsea to use to extinguish any fires that I managed to accidentally start.

"Your first lesson in being a Fire Elemite is being a torch. Basically you catch your hand on fire. Just do it like this." He held his hand out palm up and it burst into flames.

I held my hands palm up as I concentrated.

"Ah!" I exclaimed as a sudden puff of fire shot a couple inches into the air and burnt out a split second later.

Kyle laughed. "Don't try so hard, just let it happen."

I tried again and this time it worked.

"Look!" I said excitedly, holding out my hand. It was so amazing. I could see that my hand was on fire, but it didn't burn me, it actually made my hand colder. I put the fire out.

"Why does it make my hand colder?" I asked.

"Because the fire needs to take energy from you and the environment to start. You can't have a fire without energy. Anyways, the next lesson is throwing fire. All you do is instead of catching your hand on fire, turn the fire into a ball. Make it so it's roughly the size of a baseball. It's easier to throw that way."

I concentrated and managed to make a fireball. When I was done I looked at Kyle for further instruction.

"Ok," he continued. "You're going to want to throw towards the river and basically it's just like throwing a baseball." *Oh, great.* I thought. *I'm horrible at baseball!* I took a deep breath and threw the fireball as hard as I could.

Apparently, I had thrown it too hard because it landed on the other side of the river, catching a tree on fire. Chelsea acted quickly, running forward and making a scooping motion with her hands to create a pillar of water that she shot across the river to put out the fire.

"Oops," I said sheepishly. It was pretty embarrassing.

"That's ok," Kyle reassured me. "Let's move on to something else. Next up is changing the temperature. Let's start with changing the temperature of individual things, then the environment. Ok, so here's a rock. Now put it in your hand and heat it up."

"Umm, okay." I concentrated on heating the rock and felt it slowly warm up in my hand. I could feel the energy transferring from my hands into the rock. When it was hot, I handed it to Kyle.

"Very good," he said. "Now we got to work on changing the temperature of the environment. So just concentrate real hard and we'll tell you when we can feel a difference." I nodded and closed my eyes. I concentrated on sending some of my warmth out to the environment. I also tried bringing warmth from nearby places to us. I wasn't sure if it was working because I was getting a bit colder.

"I can feel it," Sam told me. I was getting weaker, so I stopped trying to warm it up and I immediately collapsed. I sat up and put my hand on my head. I was feeling dizzy and a bit faint. They were all kneeling beside me.

"Are you ok?" Sam asked me.

"I think so," I answered. "I just need a little rest."

"Well, I think we should be done for today," Kyle said. "That was your last lesson anyways. Get a good night sleep, Christa. You should be fine."

Sam helped me up and walked me to my car.

"I can drive myself," I protested when he took me to the passenger side.

"It would calm my nerves if I drove you home. Besides," he added, "better safe than sorry."

Even though it was a short ride home, I dozed in the car. When we got to my house, Sam offered to carry me inside, but after I insisted that I was well enough to walk, he settled on steadying me by putting an arm around my shoulder.

My mom came in from the living room as we entered.

"Hello, Mrs. McCalliston," Sam said cheerily. "Christa's a little tired. She was playing soccer with me and my family and it kind of wore her out."

"I'm fine," I insisted. "I just need a little nap before dinner."

"You were playing soccer?" my mom laughed.

"Not very well," I answered.

"That doesn't matter," Sam interjected. "We weren't keeping score."

The lie worked well, I avoided another circumstance when my secret was in potential danger. I went upstairs to my room and groaned when I realized that I had to get ready for work. I brushed my hair and grabbed my purse, then headed down the stairs and back out the door.

The next day was pretty much normal at school except Rachel was going on about our girl's night out the next day.

"It's going to be so much fun! We can go shopping at the mall and eat at that one place that we like and it's going to be so much fun!" I nodded and smiled. It's always best to let Rachel do all the talking.

During study hall, I sneezed which accidentally blew around a few more papers than a normal sneeze should have and Rachel looked at me funny. Other than that it was a pretty normal day.

After school we went back to the river to do some Water Elemite training. Chelsea was waiting for me by the shore with a big tub of water and an even bigger smile.

"This is going to be so much fun! I finally get to show you what we Water Elemites can do!"

"What's the tub of water for?" I asked. "There's a river right there."

"Well it's kind of hard to freeze running water, especially on your first try."

"Good point. So what do we do first?"

"First we'll make a simple bubble," she answered. "Start by getting your hands wet." I followed her lead and dipped my hands in the river.

"Okay," I said when I pulled my hands out of the water. "Now what?"

"Cup your hands and blow." She demonstrated by making a bowl shape with her hands and blowing across them. As she blew, a bubble grew and then broke off into the air, floating away before bursting above our heads. "Now you try."

I tried my best to do what she did, but my bubble came out sloppy and popped as soon as it left my hands.

"That's okay," she told me. "That was a great first try. Besides, your only instructions were to make a bubble, which you did. Anyways, next we're going to manipulate the water in the river."

"Okay," I said. "What exactly are we going to do?"

"First we're going to make a water ball." She walked over to the river and held out her hand, palm up. As she raised it, a water ball raised out of the river. In one swift movement, she turned and hurled the water ball right at Sam's face.

"Hey!" he complained as he wiped the water off his face with his shirt. Chelsea and I were cracking up laughing.

"Okay, your turn," she said after she calmed down a little. I took a deep breath to get out the last of the giggles, and then turned towards the river. It wasn't very hard to make a water ball and as soon as I had one, I threw it right at Chelsea who disappointed me by catching it. Then she used my own water ball against me by throwing it back and soaking the left side of my body. We got into a full-fledged water fight until Sam noticed the time and told us we'd better hurry up.

"Right," I said. "Back to business."

"Now we're going to make a current in this tub," Chelsea said. "So just concentrate and move your hand in the direction you want it to go." She moved her hand in a circular motion over the tub and the water started moving and turning until it was a whirlpool that took up the entire tub. She stopped moving her hand and the water calmed until it became almost completely still. She smiled at me encouragingly and I stretched my hand out over the tub. I moved my hand up and down in a wavelike motion and the water responded by making miniature waves that crashed into the sides of the tub.

"Very good. Now we're going to freeze it, then melt it, and then vaporize it. It's so much fun, I'll show you." She stretched her hand out over the tub and frost began to form on the edges. Ice spread out from the sides until the entire tub was frozen solid. Then she made a swift motion with her hand over the tub and it all melted almost immediately. She smiled at me. "Now the water's nice and cold for you, so this should be easy." I stretched my hand over the tub and the water once again began to freeze. "Okay, now unfreeze it," she said. "It's a little trickier." I tried it and she was right. It took me a little while to unthaw it completely, but eventually I did.

"Okay, so what about vaporizing? I mean, I did it once with Sam in a puddle, but I'm not sure what I did exactly."

"Oh, vaporizing is easy. Here I'll show you." She stretched out her hand and the water started boiling. Suddenly, the water level started rapidly decreasing and the air became thick with mist and fog. After the tub was all emptied out, she closed her hand into a fist and all the fog rushed into the tub, turning back into liquid water as it went.

"Whoa." It was so amazing I didn't even know what to think.

"Your turn!" she announced cheerfully as she gestured to the tub.

I gave it my best shot, but I only got half the tub vaporized before I got too tired and it all liquefied in midair and fell to the ground. I frowned at the tub, feeling like a failed because I didn't vaporize all the water.

"That was good," Chelsea complimented me. I could tell she was just trying to make me feel better. "You'll be vaporizing the whole tub in no time."

"Okay, well I got to get to work. I traded shifts so that I could go on that girl's night out tomorrow with you and Jen and Rachel. See you tomorrow."

Chapter 15

Suspicions

The next day, the only thing my friends and I could talk about was our girl's night out that we had planned for after school.

"So the plan is that I'll follow you home so you can ditch your car and school stuff then we'll go pick up Jen and Chelsea," Rachel was telling me. "That will give us enough time to drive there, shop, eat, and whatever else and still be able to drive back in time for curfew. By the way, when is your curfew?"

"Midnight," I answered.

"Okay, cool," Rachel responded. "Mine too. What about you guys?"

"Mine's midnight," Jenny answered.

"I don't have a curfew," said Chelsea.

"Seriously? You're lucky. Anyways, that means that we'll have time to catch a movie, too."

"Sounds like a plan. What movie do you guys want to see?"

"How about that one romantic comedy with that one actor we like?"

"Oh, I wanted to see that one!" Jen said excitedly.

"That one sounds good, let's do it," Chelsea said.

After school Rachel followed me home as planned and I ran inside to drop off my school bag in my room and grab my purse. Then I walked out the door and up to Rachel's car.

"Hey Christa, ready to go?"

"Sure thing, let's do this."

"Happy early birthday by the way."

"Thanks."

I got into her car and we went to pick up Jen and Chelsea. Then we were on our way to Portland for our first real girl's night out since Rachel got back.

We drove in to Portland and immediately headed towards the mall. Once there, we didn't waste any time. We headed straight to all our favorite stores. We tried on dozens of clothes and even bought some of them. We said "yes", "no", "definitely not", and "absolutely" every time one of us came out of the dressing room.

Finally it was time to eat. The sun was starting to go down and there were clouds in the sky, so it was getting kind of dark. We all piled into Rachel's car. She turned the key and then tried to turn the headlights on. Nothing happened.

"Dang it! My headlights must be out!" she complained, hitting the dashboard in frustration. "If I drive in this light with no headlights I'll get a ticket." Trying very hard to hide what I was doing, I snapped my fingers and the headlights turned on.

"How did you do that?" she asked.

"Do what?" I asked in the most innocent tone I could manage.

"Never mind," she said, shaking her head. "At least the headlights are on. Okay, let's go!" She pulled out of the parking space and drove out of the parking lot. I glanced back at Chelsea and her look warned me to be more careful in the future. I promised myself I'd try a little harder to remain inconspicuous.

Rachel drove us to our favorite restaurant and, since it was Chelsea's first time in Portland, we all reassured her that she would love it. We ordered dinner and then sat talking and laughing about classes, teachers, boys, clothes, the upcoming homecoming dance, and all that other girl stuff.

"So has Matt asked you out yet?" Jenny asked Rachel eagerly.

"No, but I think he's going to ask me soon," she responded. "I heard Ben talking to him and Ben said 'Just ask her out. Don't be a chicken. She's totally in to you, I can tell.' I'm just assuming he was talking about me." Rachel couldn't have looked happier if he'd asked her to marry him.

"That's so great, Ray," I told her. "I'll be right back; I have to use the restroom." I got up and walked to the bathroom.

I came out of the stall to wash my hands when suddenly I smelled something bad. And it wasn't dirty-toilets-in-a-public-bathroom bad. The scent got my adrenaline pumping. It was something that I had never smelt before, but I recognized it instinctively: Vampire. I turned to my left and saw her leaning on the wall by the sinks. She looked just like any other person you'd see walking along the sidewalk or eating dinner out in the restaurant. Something told me she was here to eat, just like me, only she wasn't interested in anything off the menu.

"Well, well, well," she said in a smooth, clear voice. "Looks like I found myself a much more satisfying snack than those disgusting humans out there. I'm going to enjoy this." She had a cocky smile on her face like she was sure she could beat me. I took a deep breath and prepared myself to fight. Adrenaline pumped through my veins and I used it to help boost my powers. The Vampire began walking slowly towards me with a hungry look in her eye. My hands burst into flames and I balled them into fists. She hesitated.

"You're one of those flame throwing ones," she said nervously. I could tell she'd been hoping I was an Animal, Air, or Earth Elemite because they wouldn't have as much to work with in a bathroom. I looked over her shoulder at the sinks and suddenly one exploded, soaking her with water.

"Are you sure you know what you're getting yourself into?" I asked, trying to sound tougher than I felt.

"How did you…?" She hesitated, unsure what to do next. She shook her head, splattering water from her hair on to the mirror. Then she started walking towards me again, but slower and more cautious. I waited until she was close enough to me before slamming a flaming fist into her face. She fell back, screaming. I let the flames on my hands go out and focused on making the fire on her face spread. When she was good and burned, I put out the fire so the restaurant wouldn't burn down. When I was all done, I noticed my hands were shaking. I took deep breaths and tried to calm down. Then I washed my hands and left the bathroom.

"Are you okay?" Rachel asked me when I got back to the table. "You were in there for a long time and you look exhausted."

"Yeah, I'm fine," I told her. "I'm a little tired, but I'm fine."

After dinner, Rachel took me aside.

"Are you okay, Chris?"

"Yeah, I'm fine."

"Are you sure?" she asked. "I'm mean, a lot of strange things have been happening around you lately and you've been acting kind of weird. Are you sure you're okay?"

"I'm fine, Ray. I just haven't been getting enough sleep lately that's all. I really appreciate you asking, though." It was a lame excuse and Rachel looked at me a little skeptically, but she didn't argue. We walked over to rejoin the others and then it was off to the movies.

After we got back, I immediately walked up to my room and got ready for bed. I was exhausted. Turns out fighting a Vampire in a restaurant bathroom can really wear you out. Once I was changed with my teeth brushed I crawled into bed and fell right to sleep. That night I dreamed of Vampires.

I was sitting in the clearing with Fatty and Max. A slight breeze blew through the clearing. I stiffened at the smell of Vampires that it brought. I stood and faced the direction it was coming from. A male Vampire with sleek black hair pulled back in a rubber band stepped out from the trees and began walking towards me. About four more followed behind him. I took a deep breath and prepared to fight them. I tried to light my hands on fire. Nothing happened. I tried to make the wind pick up so I could blow sand in their faces. Nothing happened. I tried to grow a wall of Poison Healers. Nothing happened. I began to panic. I found that I could still communicate with Fatty and Max, though. They stood with me as the Vampires got closer. They surrounded us and lunged. We fought ruthlessly, but it was five against three and they were a lot faster than Fatty and Max. I had only my brute strength and my speed to protect me. One of them lunged for my throat and I didn't have enough time to react...

I sat up suddenly, clutching my throat and breathing heavily. I looked around and realized that I was safe in my bedroom. The clock on my nightstand told me that it was two o'clock in the morning. I laid back down on my pillow and tried to remind myself it was only a dream.

Chapter 16

The Date

The next day was my birthday. I woke up and smiled to myself when I realized what day it was. I got up and got ready for my date with Sam. I put on my favorite shirt and jeans and brushed through the tangles in my hair. When I was all done getting ready, I heard a knock on the door.

When I opened the door, there he was, looking pretty darn near flawless.

"Happy Birthday," he said with a smile as he pulled out a big bouquet of multi-colored chrysanthemums, my favorite flower.

"You remembered!" I exclaimed as I took the flowers.

"Well, we've been talking about going out on your birthday for a while. You didn't think I would forget did you?" he said with a laugh.

"No, I meant the flowers. You remembered that they're my favorite."

"Of course I did," he said. "You're my girlfriend." Suddenly he stiffened.

"What?" I looked around me and down at myself, trying to see what had made him stiffen like that.

"Christa," he said slowly. "Why do you have the faint smell of Vampire on you?"

"Oh, that." I told him about the Vampire that had attacked me in the bathroom the night before.

"I'm so glad you're alright," he said with relief when I was done. He pulled me closer to him so he could wrap his arms around me. "Good thing you aren't only an Animal Elemite like me, or you wouldn't have had anything useful to work with. But still, you must have been terrified. I'm going to be keeping just a little bit closer watch on you from now on."

"Why?"

"You never know," he said. "She could have had a mate."

"Well, I guess I don't blame you. It was pretty scary," I admitted. "We should go," I added after a moment's pause. "But let me put these in some water first." He followed me into the kitchen and I found a vase. I filled it with water from the tap before arranging the chrysanthemums inside and placing it on the dining room table.

"Let's go," I said when I finished. We walked out to his truck and he opened the passenger side door for me. He pulled out of the driveway and started off down the road.

"First stop, the Portland Zoo," he said cheerfully as we drove into Portland city limits.

"Really?" I asked.

"Yeah," he answered. "Zoos are some of my favorite places. You'd think that being an Animal Elemite would make me hate seeing animals in captivity. But actually, none of the animals are unhappy with their living conditions. At least, not at any zoo I've ever visited. Plus, some of them were rescued from dangerous situations or injuries when they were brought into captivity. Actually, a lot of zoo keepers are Animal Elemites."

"The zoo sounds like a great idea, let's do it."

We walked around the zoo talking and laughing and enjoying all the exhibits. All the animals came out of their caves and nests and burrows when we walked up if they weren't already out in the open. None of the animals seemed bitter or resentful about their situation. Some of them were actually bred in captivity and so they didn't know any better.

At the lorikeet exhibit, we bought little cups of juice so the lorikeets could drink from them. One little lorikeet flew up to my cup, perched on the rim, and began to drink a little half-heartedly. It was obviously mourning the loss of something.

"What's the matter?" I asked her.

"I lost my mother this morning," she answered. *"She died of old age."*

"I'm sorry," I said, trying to comfort it. *"I know what it's like to lose a parent."*

"Do you have a father?" Sam asked. *"Why don't you talk to him? I'm sure he knows the right thing to say."*

"He seems even sadder than I am, but I'll give it a shot." With that, the beautiful little lorikeet flew off into the trees of the exhibit.

After the zoo, we went to lunch then caught a movie. The movie was some sappy romantic comedy, but I loved it. I guess girls are just like that.

"Did you like the movie?" Sam asked as we walked out of the theater, hand in hand.

"I loved it! You?"

"The truth?"

I laughed. "It's okay. Boys aren't *supposed* to like romantic comedies. It's how the world works."

He laughed with me. "That sounds about right. So where do you want to go for dinner?"

"I don't know. There're a lot of good places."

"Well, you have to choose because I've only been to Portland once before, so I don't know where all the good restaurants are."

"Well, I'm not sure what I feel like eating yet." Eventually, after debating a little, we were able to decide on a restaurant.

After we ate, Sam drove us home and I dozed in the car. I hadn't been getting nearly enough sleep lately and training was taking a lot out of me. I guess it was all just catching up to me. The next thing I knew, Sam was waking me up and telling me we were home. I looked around dazed and realized that we were parked in front of my house.

"Oh, sorry about that. I didn't mean to fall asleep. I'll see you tomorrow." I leaned over and kissed him goodbye before turning to open the door.

"See ya," he answered as I climbed out of the car.

I went into the house and climbed the stairs to my bedroom. I changed into sweats and a t-shirt, crawled into bed, and fell immediately to sleep.

Chapter 17

Airborne

When I woke up the next morning, I felt perfectly rejuvenated. I dressed in jeans and a sweat shirt before descending the stairs to breakfast. I popped some bread in the toaster and poured myself some juice. When I was done with breakfast, I pulled on some shoes before heading out to the woods to meet Sam and Brian.

"Where's Brian?" I asked when I got there. "I thought we were going to do some Air Elemite training." Sam and Chelsea were standing in the clearing, but Brian wasn't anywhere in sight.

"He had some last minute homework to finish up, but he'll be here later," Sam answered. "So I thought that Chelsea and I could teach you some fighting techniques while we wait."

"Sounds good. What do we do first?" I was nervous about learning how to fight, but the incident with the Vampire in the restroom made me feel like it was the right thing to do.

"First I'll teach you how to throw a punch. Your flaming fists are going to make your punches much more effective than mine could ever be, but you still need to learn good form. It makes for a more powerful punch." I nodded to show that I was listening and understood. "What you need to do is stand with your feet apart and turn your body with the punch. So twist your body back like this when you pull back your arm and then put your whole body weight into it. I'll demonstrate a punch on Chelsea."

Suddenly he threw a punch right at Chelsea's face, but she dodged it easily. They both moved impossibly fast, but my enhanced eyesight caught every move.

"Of course," said Sam, "if I was really trying to hit her, I could have, but I didn't want to hurt her."

"You couldn't hit the inside of a barn," she retorted.

"Is that a challenge?" She just rolled her eyes in response.

"Now you try, Christa," she told me.

"Um, ok." I tried my best at a punch, but Chelsea still dodged it with ease.

"Pull your arm back more and don't be so stiff," she instructed. I tried again and still missed, but I got closer this time.

"Was that good?" I asked.

"It was great," she replied. "Now I'm going to let you hit me so I can feel how much power you got."

"Maybe that's not such a good idea, Chelsea," Sam interjected. "Maybe she should punch me instead."

"If you want to volunteer, then go ahead."

"Are you sure?" I asked him.

"Yep," he replied. "And don't hold back. I need to know how well you can pack a punch."

"Alright, here goes nothing." I pulled back my arm and punched him in the stomach as hard as I could.

"Oof!" he exclaimed, doubling over in pain and clutching his stomach.

"Oh my gosh, are you alright?" I cried, reaching down to help him. Suddenly he grinned and straightened up.

"Yeah, I'm just messing with you," he laughed. "You're so gullible. That was a pretty good punch, though."

"You jerk!" I said, playfully hitting him on the shoulder. "Do you really think it was a good punch?"

"Yeah," he said. "I could sense you were holding back, though. I just hope you don't hold back in a Vampire attack."

"Well, it's hard to go all out when I'm punching someone I like, but since I don't like Vampires, I don't think it will be a problem." Just then I heard a car coming.

"Someone's driving down the road," said Chelsea.

"Let's see who it is," Sam said. Whoever it was parked the car and got out.

"Brian!" Chelsea cried. Suddenly they were both at the top of the hill and Brian put his arm around her.

"How did you know it was Brian before we could even see him?" I asked.

"You need to learn how to use your nose, Christa," she replied.

"Are you ready to learn some Air Elemite skills?" Brian asked.

"You bet."

"Alright, first we're going to learn how to make air currents, or in other words, wind," he said. "First you need to concentrate on the air around you. Clear your mind and concentrate."

I took a deep breath. "Alright."

"Next you need to think of the way you want the air to move. At first, it's easier to move your hands the way you want the currents to go, but when you get used to your powers, you'll be able to move the air without moving your body at all. Here, let me show you." He began moving his hands in a swooping motion to the left and the wind began moving in the exact same way. "Concentrate on how hard you want the wind to blow, too." The wind began picking up and then it suddenly died down again.

"Alright, I'll give it a try," I replied. I closed my eyes and concentrated. I pictured the way I wanted the wind to blow. Then I began moving my hands in a swooping motion. I could feel the wind begin to follow my hands. As I moved my hands faster, the wind picked up. I slowed down my hands and the wind got softer.

"Wow, that was great for your first try," Brian said. "Now we'll make tornadoes. They're not really tornadoes, because they're not big enough. They're more like mini whirl winds. Anyways, it's the same concept as before, only don't use your hands because that actually makes it more difficult. Just imagine the tornado in front of you and make sure you don't make it too big or you might lose control of it and that would be bad. I'll show you how it's done."

A mini tornado began to form in front of him and grow. It quickly grew to be ten feet tall before it stopped growing. Brian sent it on a trip around the clearing before bringing it back to him and terminating it.

"Wow that was really cool," I said.

"Go ahead and try it."

My first attempt was pretty feeble. My next attempt was a little strong and I needed Brian's help to destroy it. Finally, I was able to make one that was perfect. It made me feel so powerful to be able to control a tornado, even if it was a small one. I played around with it for a second or two before getting rid of it.

"Alright," Brian said. "I'll let you rest for a minute before we move on to our next lesson: flying."

I sat down on the ground and took a drink out of the water bottle I had been smart enough to bring. Sam came and sat down next to me.

"You're doing awesome," he said. "You'll be an expert at all this stuff in no time."

"Thanks," I said.

"No I mean it. You have to learn so many more skills than other Elemites because you can control all the Elements. But even with so much more stuff to learn, you're still getting the hang of it faster than any of us ever did."

"He's right Christa," Chelsea agreed. "You amaze me."

"Thanks guys," I said, blushing from all the praise. I wasn't sure what else to say. "I think I'm ready to start flying now."

"Alright," said Brian. "In theory, flying is easy, but putting it into practice is really hard, so don't get discouraged if you don't get it the first time. Basically you just manipulate the air around you so that it holds you up and makes you float. I'll show you." He made the air currents swoop down and then created an updraft that lifted him into the air. He flew around a bit, effortlessly changing the air currents to keep himself up.

"Looks easy enough," I said, although I didn't actually believe that. I used the air currents the same way he did and managed to get myself a few inches off the ground. I hovered there for a moment and then wobbled a bit before falling back to the ground. I sighed and looked over at Brian. He had also landed, but it wasn't because he couldn't keep himself up.

"That was a good first try," he said. "How about I hold your hand and help you fly up a bit higher so you can get used to it? Then you can start in the air which will give you more room to make your updraft. Maybe it will be a bit easier after that."

"Alright," I answered. "Let's give it a shot." Brian took my hand and began to fly upwards, pulling me along with him. Once we were about ten feet up, he stopped rising higher and just hovered.

"Okay, now try keeping yourself up. I'll be right here ready to catch you and, given the small chance that I don't, Sam and Chelsea are my backups. Besides, we're not that high up and the grass is really soft."

Somehow, his words did little to comfort me. I took a few deep breaths to calm myself down as I tried to steady myself. I began trying to create an updraft strong enough to keep me hovering. As I started to get the hang of it, Brian slowly let me go.

"Look!" I cried in excitement. "I'm doing it!" I was a little wobbly, but I had good balance for the most part. Brian helped me go even higher until we were twenty feet off the ground. I was about to try going forward when we heard another car coming down the road.

Chapter 18

Caught

"Someone's coming," said Brian in an urgent tone of voice.

From my elevated height I could see over the hill to the road. I looked over and saw that the car that was coming was one I knew well. It was Rachel's. She was pulling off the road and into the patch of dirt and grass where Sam, Brian, and I had parked.

"Oh no," I breathed. I couldn't let her see me flying. Panicking and losing my concentration, I lost my balance and began to wobble dangerously in the air until Brian steadied me by putting a hand on my shoulder.

"Let's go," he said.

Brian guided me back to the ground as quickly as he could with Sam helping me to land in the end. I landed back on the ground just in time for us all to turn and see Rachel coming down the hill. She walked over to us with a surprised expression on her face.

"Um, hey Ray," I said nervously.

"You – up – sky – flying!" she managed to stutter, pointing at me and then up at the sky, looking totally bewildered.

"What do you mean, Ray? Flying? That's crazy." I knew I didn't sound convincing. I'd never been a very good liar. People always told me it was a good thing, but in this situation, it definitely wasn't.

"Christa Ellen McCalliston, don't you dare lie to me!! I saw you up in the sky from the other side of the hill! You were up in the sky with Brian! Then you started coming back down and I ran to the top of the hill just in time to see you land! Tell me the truth! What's been going on lately? I mean it's not just this time. I mean, now that I think of it, a lot of weird things have been happening lately. Like when that bird ate out of your hand and when you were the only one not cold because you were radiating warmth. Then there was the time my headlights were out and I could've sworn you like snapped your fingers or something and turned them back on. And that stuff was weird and all, but I probably would've just shaken them off and said it was all in my head if it wasn't for this. What's going on? Do you not trust me enough to tell me or something?"

"It's not like that! It's not like that at all! I wanted to tell you! I really did! But…I mean, it was just—" I tried to explain, but she wasn't listening. She interrupted me again to continue with her angry rant.

"I came out here because I was worried about you," she said. "I was going to stop by your house and see if you wanted to hang out or something, but your mom said you were at the Campton's. So I called their house because if you were with Chelsea, then I wanted to ask if I could hang, too. And if you were with Sam, then I didn't want to get in the way of your boyfriend/ girlfriend stuff, so I would just ask if Chelsea wanted to hang with me. But Tasha said that none of you were there. And she wouldn't tell me where you were. So I thought that maybe you had come out here again. I thought you had quit doing that a few years ago, but I thought that maybe you had turned into an emotional wreck again or something and came out here to mourn for your dad, so I came out here to comfort you. But I guess you aren't emotionally unstable. You're just keeping secrets!"

"Ray, it's not that I don't trust you, because I do. It's just that I couldn't tell you. I really, really wanted to, but I'm not supposed to. I mean, I'm not allowed to. But if you meet me at my house in a couple of hours, I'll tell you everything. I promise. We just need a chance to cool down and I need a chance to get everything straight before I say anything. This is a lot more complicated than you think. Please," I pleaded, "just trust me."

"Alright," she said reluctantly, eyeing me carefully. "I'll be there." Then she walked back up the hill to her car.

I waited until I heard her start heading down the road before I turned to Sam. He looked just as worried as I felt.

"What do I do?" I asked. "I'm not supposed to reveal the secret, but she caught me! And how am I supposed to explain it to her without making her feel like I betrayed her by keeping a secret? We never keep secrets from each other! I totally understand how she's feeling and I don't know how to make it better."

"I'm not sure how to handle this, Christa," he answered sadly. "I guess the best way is to just tell her the truth and we'll worry about the Elders later. Right now it looks like your only option. I'm sorry. I know you don't need any more added stress right now."

I nodded, thankful for his concern and knowing that he was probably right. Then I began walking slowly back to my car.

Chapter 19

A Really Hard Explanation

As I drove back to my house I was thinking about what I was going to say to Rachel. When I got there, I walked upstairs to my room, fell down on my bed, and stared at the ceiling. What was I going to do? The secret was pretty much out, so I'd just have to tell the truth.

I didn't realize how much time had passed until I heard a knock on the door. I went back downstairs and let Rachel inside, ushering her into the living room.

"Alright, now spill," she said as soon as we were seated on the couch. I took a deep breath and decided to just jump right in.

"I have the power to control the Elements," I said. "Fire, Water, Air, Earth, and also Animals. When you saw me in the clearing earlier, I was learning how to use my powers over air so that I could fly. I also have superhuman strength, speed, eyesight, hearing, and smell."

"How long have you had these powers?" she asked incredulously. "I've known you for, like, ever! How could I have not known about this?!"

"I only got my powers recently," I answered. "There's a name for someone with powers like me. We are called Elemites. Elemites are like humans, only we live a little longer and we have special powers. When we get our powers, the aging process slows down by about half. An Elemite's powers usually come in when they are between the ages of fifteen and eighteen, but even fifteen is considered pretty young."

"So where do Sam and the rest of the Campton's fit into all of this? I know they're in on the secret."

"Sam and his family all have powers like me, just not as many. In fact, I'm not a normal Elemite. Most Elemites can only control one Element, but I can control all of them."

"Whoa," she said with awe, forgetting for a moment that she was mad at me. "That's pretty awesome. But wait, none of this explains why you kept it a secret."

"Besides following human laws, Elemites also have leaders who make laws for us and the biggest one is keeping the secret. You have to get permission to tell someone the secret. I was going to get permission to tell you, but I wanted to make sure I knew enough about this world myself before bringing anyone else into it. I'm sorry Rachel. I really was going to tell you."

"Oh," she said, sounding like she was feeling a little guilty for being mad. "So are you going to get in trouble now?"

I shook my head slowly and shrugged my shoulders. "I don't know. But I'll try to make sure everything turns out all right."

"Christa, I'm sorry," she said, giving me a hug. "I shouldn't have gotten mad. You had a good reason to keep that secret from me and I should've just trusted that you had a reason. I'm sorry."

"It's alright. If our roles were reversed, I probably would've gotten mad, too. Besides, you trusted me enough to come listen to my explanation instead of just stomping off all mad and never talking to me again."

She laughed. "That's true. Hey, can I see some of the cool stuff you do with your powers?"

"Well, I'm pretty tired from using them today, but Sam and I are going to go practice some more tomorrow if you want to come."

"Alright. Same place I caught you at today?"

"Yep."

"I'll be there."

"Oh yeah, are there any other magical things in the world besides Elemites?"

"Oh yeah."

"Really? Like what?"

"Vampires, Elves, Poison Healer plants, Mermaids, Unicorns, Fairies, Pixies, Dragons, Griffins, and Giants."

"Seriously? How could I miss that kind of stuff? You'd think I'd notice them or something."

"They remain hidden," I explained. "They're not supposed to reveal the secret either."

"Really? That sucks. What's with all the secrecy?"

"I think it's because humans would think we were freaks or try to exploit our powers or get scared of us and try to kill us. Remember in the olden days when they used to hunt down Vampires and stuff? And I bet the supposed 'witches' in the Salem witch trials were actually like Elemites and Elves and stuff. The humans just didn't understand their powers. And I'm sure some of them were innocent humans wrongly accused because of widespread fear."

"You're right, that would be bad. But what are magical creatures like?" she asked eagerly.

"I haven't actually met any of them yet except for a Vampire, but Sam told me all about them."

"Well, I still want to hear what you know. And you met a Vampire? When? Was it scary?"

"It was when we did that girl's night out. We were at the restaurant and I went to go use the bathroom. When I came out of the stall to wash my hands, she was standing there staring at me. She told me I smelled a lot better than the things on the menu. One thing you got to know about Vampires is that even though human blood is very appealing to them, Elemite blood drives them crazy. They'll go out of their way to hunt one of us down. So I had to kill her right there in the bathroom."

"That's why you came out of the bathroom looking all shaken up. So how did you kill her?"

"I weakened her with water from the faucets and then I burnt her with fire that I made myself."

"What do you mean you weakened her with water?"

"Water weakens Vampires. And fire is one of the things that can kill them."

"That's sweet. I can't believe you killed a Vampire!"

"I can hardly believe it myself."

"Oh my gosh, I got to go," she said suddenly, looking at the time on her phone. "You don't know how much I wish I could stay here and listen to you tell me about mystical creatures and stuff, but I got to go run some errands for my mom. See you tomorrow."

The next day in history I told Sam what happened with Rachel.

"So she took it well?" he asked.

"Yeah," I replied. "And she wants to come watch us practice today."

"Fair enough."

"Now we just got to figure out what to do about the Elders."

"I'm sure they'll understand," he reassured me, but he didn't look very sure.

Chapter 20

And the Chase Begins

After school that day, we all met up at the clearing. Rachel was really excited about seeing what I could do. She talked about it nonstop all during study hall.

"Okay, I'm ready," she said after walking over the hill and into the clearing. "What are you going to do first?"

"Well, I kind of need to practice all of the Elements, so which one are you most excited to see?" I asked.

"Can you show me how you make fire with your hands?" she asked excitedly.

"Alright." I held out my hands and instantly lit them on fire. Rachel stared with wide eyes as the flames licked my palms, but didn't burn me.

"That is so freaking cool!" she said with amazement. "Doesn't it hurt?"

"No. It doesn't burn me. But it would burn you, so don't touch," I answered as she slowly reached her hand out as if she wanted to touch the flames.

"That is so cool. What else can you do?"

"Pay attention to the temperature of the air around you," I told her as I extinguished my hands and focused on drawing in heat from the surrounding air. After about ten seconds, she shivered.

"That's amazing! Can you make it warmer, too?"

"Yep," I smiled. I began warming the air back up to normal and then kept going, making it unusually warm before bringing it back down to where it was supposed to be.

"That's insane. Hey, can you fly now? I didn't really get to see it very well when I caught you before."

"Well, I just learned how to do that and it's not really safe for me to try it without Brian here. But he'll be here soon so I can practice some more."

"So does he, like, have power over the Air and stuff?"

"Yeah," I answered. "He is what we call an Air Elemite."

"So what's your power?" she asked, turning to Sam. "No wait! Let me guess. Um Fire? Water? Earth? Alright, just tell me."

"I am an Animal Elemite," he answered. "I can influence animals and heal them."

"That's awesome. Can you guys show me that now?"

"Sure," I replied. I closed my eyes and searched for Fatty and Max with my mind. I connected my mind to theirs and called them to me. After a few seconds, I opened my eyes again and smiled. "Fatty and Max are coming."

"Who are Fatty and Max?" Rachel asked. "And what kind of a name is Fatty?"

"You'll see." Just then I heard something in the trees off to my right.

"I hear something," said Sam.

"Me too."

"What? I don't hear anything," Rachel said with a frown. Then she gasped. "Is it Fatty and Max? Are they here already?"

Sam shook his head. "They couldn't have gotten here that fast and it didn't sound like them anyway."

"Oh."

"It was coming from over here," I said, leading Sam and Rachel over to the edge of the clearing. We stepped into the trees and kept walking for a few yards. What we found was a bunny with his ears caught in a thorn bush.

"I knew I heard something," said Sam, reaching down and untangling the bunny.

"It has scratches on its ears," I said reaching over and gently placing a hand on the scratches. When I took my hand away, his ears were as good as new. Rachel watched the whole thing with amazement.

"That is so cool that I don't even know what to say," she said. "Can I hold him?"

"I guess so," Sam answered, handing her the bunny.

"Let's go back to the clearing," I suggested. We all walked back together while Rachel carried the bunny, stroking its ears the whole way.

When we entered the clearing, we saw Fatty and Max coming out of the trees on the other side. Rachel gasped and began to tremble with fear. The bunny got nervous and jumped out of her arms, running off into the forest.

"It's okay," I told her. "This is Fatty and Max."

"Fatty and Max are bears?!" she asked incredulously.

"That's what I said."

"They're really friendly," Sam added. "Especially when they're with an Animal Elemite."

I walked over and rubbed Fatty on the head, right between the ears. Then I scratched Max under the chin.

"Do you want to come pet them?" I asked.

"Um," she said, unsure of herself. "I guess so." She walked over slowly and put her hand on Max's side. He turned to look at her and then stuck out his tongue and licked her in the face. She stumbled backwards a few steps, a look of total shock on her face. Sam and I just laughed.

We heard a car pull up and looked over to see Brian coming over the hill.

"There you are!" I greeted him. "I was beginning to think you weren't going to show up."

"Well, I'm here, so let's get started," he said.

"This is going to be so cool," said Rachel.

"Why don't we start off pretty easy," Brian continued. He pushed off the ground and flew up about seven or eight feet in the air. "Just try flying up to here. Push off the ground to get yourself started. Just jump."

I concentrated on the updraft I wanted and then jumped. I shot into the air, easily matching Brian's height. I let out a surprised laugh and then experimented with going from side to side. Then I got a little braver and went a little higher. I twirled once and then decided to try doing a lap around the clearing.

I wobbled a bit at first before finding my balance. I started out slowly, then gradually got a little faster.

"I can't believe I'm doing it!" I cried.

"Me neither!" said Rachel.

"You're doing really well," Brain commented.

I experimented some more with going faster, flying higher, and doing tricks like loop de loops and coming out of dives. But eventually I got tired and had to come back down for a rest.

"You are unbelievable, Christa," said Rachel. "This is all so exciting!"

"I know, even I can hardly believe some of the stuff I can do with my powers." Suddenly we heard a beep coming from her pocket.

"Oh, sorry," she apologized, taking her phone out of her pocket and reading the text she had just received. "Oh man, it's my mom. I got to go. Bye Chris! See you tomorrow!" Then she ran over the hill to her car.

"I should probably go, too," said Brian.

"Okay, thanks for the training," I told him. "See you around."

"Anytime, Christa. See ya."

"Let's get back to training," Sam said when he was gone.

Suddenly he froze. Then I caught the smell of something that instinctively made me tense up: Vampire.

One by one they started showing themselves in the clearing. I counted six. I thanked my lucky stars that Rachel had already left. She didn't need to have to deal with this.

"What is *that*?!" The closest one was the one who had spoken. He was one of four males and had sleek black hair pulled back with a rubber band. I gasped when I realized that he was the one from the dream I had about Vampires attacking me, Fatty, and Max. None of the others looked familiar.

"That is the most delicious and delightful smell that my nose has ever encountered in my entire existence—and I've lived for three hundred years," he continued.

"I believe it's coming from the girl," said another. She was the closest of the two females, but still farther back than the male who had spoken.

"Ah yes, and I believe it is the same smell from the bathroom, but you smell much better in person, my dear," he said with an unsettling smile. "You see, I came here to get revenge because you killed my mate. But I think I'm going to get a lot more pleasure out of this than I thought."

That's when I realized that in that one moment, I went from being the most powerful Elemite in the world to being the most endangered Elemite in the world. Then several things happened in a row, and I was barely able to catch all of them. First, Sam slid me behind him so he could protect me. Second, I scraped my arm on the branch of the tree behind me. The tiniest drop of blood came from the scrape, but it was enough for every single Vampire to turn their heads and stare at it with flat black eyes. All of the Vampires started running for us at once. I felt Sam's hand wrap around mine and we started running. As we raced through the trees, Sam pulled out his cell phone and pressed a button before putting it to his ear.

"Tasha," he murmured into the phone. His face was worried and serious and angry all at the same time. "We need help. Gather the others. It's a Vampire attack." He kept his tone even, but I could hear the tension in it. He took the phone away from his ear and put it back in his pocket.

"Do you think we can outrun them?" I asked.

"I don't know," he answered honestly. "We're definitely faster, but we can get tired. They can't. And I can smell ten of them."

"Ten?!" I screamed. I was still getting used to my senses, so I only smelled eight. And there were only six that were visible in the clearing. Well this was just great. Now I had *ten* psychotic Vampires chasing me. Would it never end? I wanted so badly to fly right now. I wanted to just shoot up into the air and fly away. The problem was that my powers weren't yet strong enough to carry me *and* Sam and I wasn't about to leave him behind. Suddenly I thought of an idea that made me stop in my tracks. Sam skidded to a halt not too far ahead of me and came jogging back to where I stood.

"Come on, Christa!" he pleaded, pulling me by the hand. "We don't have time! We have to go!"

"Wait a second," I told him. "I'm buying us time." I turned towards the place the Vampires were coming from, raised a humongous cloud of dust, and blew it towards them with one hundred mile an hour winds.

"Send Fatty and Max after them!" I screamed over the wind. He nodded and closed his eyes to concentrate. Fatty and Max appeared on the trail after a couple of seconds. I had switched to growing a wall of Poison Healer plants to block the way. I gave Fatty and Max specific instructions to not let the Vampires get past them if they made it through the ring of poisonous plants I made around them.

I made a ditch in the ground that ran along the line of Poison Healers and filled it with water. That one was really difficult because I had to take the water out of the air and call it up from under the ground. I didn't want to burn the forest down, so I didn't bother making a ring of fire. Then I ran off into the forest with Sam, trying to get as far away as possible from the army of Vampires that was following us.

Chapter 21

The Plan

After leaving a few decoy trails with drops of my blood to throw them off, Sam and I finally made it back to his house without any Vampires following. Everyone was waiting for us in the living room with worried expressions on their faces.

"What's the plan?" I asked, panting from our run through the forest.

"We'll call some old friends and see if they can help us," Tasha answered. "If they can, we'll establish a meeting point and then hold them off until they arrive. But even if they can help, this is a dangerous game we're playing."

"The plan sounds good to me," Brian said, nodding his head in agreement. "Call 'em up. We need all the help we can get."

"I agree," said Chelsea.

"You know others like us?" I asked.

"Sure," Kyle answered. "They're kind of like Tasha's in-laws because they're my old family. It's my brother, my sister, and my sister-in-law. They live in Portland, which is only a twenty minute run northwest from here. But we may not even be able to afford that much time."

"Really? It only takes twenty minutes? The drive is a lot longer."

"Yeah, but they can go sixty miles per hour the whole way. Plus they can go in a straight line. They don't have to follow a road."

"Right," I replied, feeling a little stupid for not realizing that myself.

"I'll call them right now," said Kyle, pulling out his phone. We all waited while he talked to his brother. After briefly explaining the situation to him, he hung up the phone and put it back in his pocket. "Tom and Cara will be here soon and they'll pick up Meg along the way."

"Okay, now we need to think of a battle plan," Sam said. "There's so many of them and they've already smelled Christa's blood, so there's no way we could run away from them forever. Our best shot is to just stand and face them. We need to kill them now before they can hurt anybody. That means that we need to decide what will give us the best advantage while keeping the Vampires away from innocent bystanders."

"I say we lure them into the woods so that we're as far away from other people as possible and then surround them," Brian suggested.

"That's a good idea," Tasha agreed. "Now we just need to coordinate who goes where so that it will all turn out perfectly. We only get one shot at this. We don't want to fail."

We spent the next fifteen minutes coordinating battle formations so that we'd be able to lead them into our trap. It was decided that Sam and I would be the ones leading them away while the others went around behind to trap them. I was a bit nervous about this, but it only made sense considering I was the one they were after.

Then, finally, Kyle's family showed up, panting from their long run. There were three of them and they all looked young and fit. One was a man with brown hair like Kyle's who looked like he was in his mid-twenties. The other two were women. One of them bore a striking resemblance to Kyle and looked like she was only a few years older than me. The other looked like she was about the same age as Kyle, but looked nothing like him with long blond hair and bright blue eyes.

"Man, what a run," said the man. "I must be out of shape. Hey, who's this? I don't think I've ever seen you before."

"This is my girlfriend Christa," Sam answered, gesturing to me.

"Well, nice to meet you, Christa," said the man, shaking my hand firmly. "I'm Tom Jones, Kyle's brother."

"I'm Cara, Tom's wife," the blond woman said with a smile.

"And I'm Megan, Tom and Kyle's sister," added the other woman. "But you can call me Meg for short."

"So is she the one you were telling me about, Kyle?" Tom asked. "The one who can control all five Elements?"

"That's me," I answered.

"That's amazing," he said with wonder in his voice. "I've never heard of anything like it."

"Alright, what's the plan?" asked Meg. We filled them in on the plan and told them what we wanted them to do. It was definitely dangerous, but they all agreed to it.

"Sounds good," Cara said.

"Yeah, but it is a little risky," Meg added.

"Any plan involving a Vampire attack is a little risky," Tom reminded her.

"True."

"We need to hurry and put our plan into action," said Sam. "It's only a matter of time before they find the real trail and make their way here."

"Right," I agreed. I was really nervous about what we were about to do, but I tried to put on a brave face. "Let's go."

Chapter 22

Trapped

When we were all ready and had everything all planned out, Tasha, Kyle, and Meg left the house first. We wished them good luck and then watched them run off towards the forest. Then Sam and I left a few minutes later. I didn't get to see them off, but I knew that Tom, Cara, Chelsea, and Brian were scheduled to leave a couple minutes after us. Grandpa George would stay behind. He was getting old and we didn't want him getting hurt.

The plan was that Sam and I would be the bait that would lure the Vampires into our trap. We were supposed to lead them straight to Tasha, Kyle, and Meg. We had a designated meeting point and they were going the long way around so they could come from the front. Sam and I were taking a more direct route. Tom, Cara, Chelsea, and Brian were supposed to bring up the rear, blocking the Vampires' escape. We were going to surround them. It was the best advantage we could think of and we didn't have a lot of time to think up any alternatives, so it was our only shot at success.

Soon after we left, the Vampires caught my scent and began to give chase. I tried really hard not to freak out and instead focused on making it to Tasha, Meg, and Kyle. Sam must have noticed the panic in my expression because he squeezed my hand reassuringly. `

"It'll be alright," he told me. I took a deep breath and nodded.

We continued running until we finally made it to the meeting spot where Tasha, Meg, and Kyle were waiting. It was a small clearing similar to the one we normally went to only smaller and farther away from town and the road. We didn't want any innocent bystanders to get dragged into the middle of this. The ground was a little more level in this clearing and there was a thicker wall of trees surrounding it, making it easier for us to block off their escape once we got them there.

"You guys okay?" Tasha asked. We could tell that they had just gotten there only a few moments before us.

"Yeah, we're fine," Sam replied. Just then, the Vampires caught up to us. They came running in at full speed and stopped about four yards away. They didn't look tired at all from the run, but their hair looked windswept and their clothes looked slightly rumpled.

Tom, Cara, Chelsea, and Brian closed in on them from behind so that we had them surrounded. All their escapes were blocked.

But something was very wrong with this picture and I had a feeling that something was about to go wrong with our plan.

There were only three Vampires. There had been six in the clearing before and Sam had smelled ten. Looking at the situation it would appear as if we had the upper hand, but I knew that things were not always what they seemed.

"Well, well, well," chuckled the Vampire that had addressed us before. He was also the same one that I had seen in my dream. He had a crooked smile and long white fangs that glistened menacingly in the sunlight. "It seems we have finally caught up with our dinner."

"You're outnumbered," I told him, trying to sound more confident than I felt. "And we have you surrounded."

His mouth stretched into a smile that sent a chill down my back.

"Oh really?" he asked. "There are nine of you and ten of us. You're only surrounding the three of us while seven of our friends are surrounding *you*."

As if on cue, seven Vampires stepped silently out of the trees around us with smug expressions on their faces. He was right; we were surrounded.

I was horrorstricken. I couldn't believe it. We had tried to set a trap and ended up falling into one instead. Our situation looked very grim at the moment.

I looked over at Sam and he looked back at me with a sad expression on his face. I gave his hand a little squeeze and turned back to the Vampires.

"You might as well just come quietly," the lead Vampire continued with a triumphant grin stretched across his devilish face. "As you can see, there's little hope left for you and your loved ones."

I got angry now. These people were willing to risk everything for me and for each other and he was really suggesting that I just give up and let him have them?

I let go of Sam's hand and took a step forward, standing tall. My hands clenched into fists and I set them on fire. I looked the Vampire in the eye and took a deep breath and breathed out sharply before speaking.

"Even if there was no hope left, I would never go down without a fight."

Chapter 23

The Stunning Truth

He stared at me coldly for a moment before replying.

"A feisty one, eh? Well, I guess you can have it your way. You know, you look oddly familiar." His tone was casual. He said it like we were strangers who had just met in the park. Suddenly he snapped his fingers, realizing why he recognized me. "That's it! It was seven years ago. Vampires have an excellent memory, so I never forget a face. He was older than you, but he had your nose, your eyes, and your skin tone. Plus he had a similar tint to his scent, but don't worry, you smell much better. He was quite tasty, but difficult to catch. He was very skilled at using bears to help fight me off." I listened, horrorstruck. It couldn't be. It was impossible. There was just no way…

"What?" I managed to mouth. "Are you saying…It was you? But, that's impossible…it couldn't be…Could it?"

"Does all of this sound familiar to you?" he asked with an amused smile. "Well, he could be related to you. It depends. I mean I have been hunting in Oregon for a while. If the facts all add up, then yes, he most likely was related to you. Now I'm just hoping that you'll be just as tasty. Or tastier."

He took a step forward. I dropped into a defensive crouch. He hesitated and seemed to think about the best angle to attack. Suddenly everyone was facing off with one of the Vampires. Kyle and Tom teamed up together to take on three of them. I was left facing the leader.

My mom was right. One moment *can* make a difference. It can change everything. One moment, I'm enjoying my senior year of high school and the next I'm defending myself from a horrible monster. My whole life was changed in just one instant. If I had blinked, I would have missed it.

I looked into the eyes of the blood-thirsty monster before me. This was just between me and him. I knew how I *wanted* it to end—with him gone and everyone I loved left alive—I just didn't know how it was *going* to end. Besides, I wasn't just fighting for my own life; I was fighting for someone so much more important to me than that. If I lost him, I lost my will to live—especially if I could have prevented it. My heart thudded wildly in my chest and my palms were sweaty. As I stood, desperately searching for a weakness in his defenses, I found myself wondering, why me? Why does it have to be me?

Time seemed to move slower and slower as we stared each other down, cautiously waiting for the other to lower their defenses. It was as if time was purposefully creeping along, just so I could be driven insane with the suspense. In reality it was probably only a few seconds, but it felt like an eternity. The atmosphere was so tense that I could almost feel it pressing in around me. Then, finally, he made a decision. He had either decided that he knew where my weak spot was, or he was tired of waiting and was going to try to kill me anyways. He started to make a lunge for my throat. In another moment, I realized that I had less than a second to react. To defend myself.

I used my powers to lift water out of a nearby puddle and hurl it at his face. He stopped mid-leap and glared at me. He tried to leap again, but he was weaker. This time I held out flaming hands. He retreated a couple of steps, not wanting to get burnt by the flames. I picked up a moss-covered rock, caught it on fire, and threw it as hard as I could at his face. Bull's-eye! He howled in pain and immediately began to try and put out the fire. I risked a glance at the rest of my friends. They all seemed to be winning their battles. Brian had already killed his Vampire and was now helping Chelsea to fight hers. Sam was doing well against his Vampire with some help from Fatty and Max. Tasha and Meg were working together to fight off two Vampires and Tom and Kyle had beaten one of the three they were fighting and were now working on the other two. Cara was just finishing off her Vampire and headed over to Tasha and Meg to help them with theirs. I smiled. We just might all survive this.

When I looked back over at my Vampire, I saw that he had managed to put out the fire, but he had a nasty burn on his face. He ran towards me and we ended up wrestling. I managed to get him on the ground and used water that I summoned from nearby puddles to weaken him. Because of that, he didn't have enough strength to break free when I commanded some tree roots to wrap around his wrists and ankles, holding him down.

"Christa!" Chelsea called. I looked over and saw that she was pointing into the forest. "Some of them got away!"

I looked around. There were only five Vampires left fighting, including the leader that I had pinned down. But there were only three bodies in the clearing. What happened to the other two? Where had they gone?

Chapter 24

Don't Even Go There

I heard a chuckle and looked down to see it was coming from the Vampire leader that was being held by tree roots. He had an evil look in his eye like he knew something that I didn't know.

"They went to go follow your scent somewhere else," he said. "They knew it might lead them to some more of your tasty friends." I thought about what that meant. If they followed my scent, that would lead them to the house.

"Collin," I whispered. He was home all alone today.

I slammed a flaming fist into the Vampire's face, catching his whole head on fire. Then I started running as fast as I could through the trees. I ran at least a mile before I remembered that I could fly. Leaping into the air, I took off as fast as I could. I shot like a rocket through the sky, traveling faster than I ever had. All I could think the whole way was, *Not my little brother. Not him. Don't hurt him.* Please *don't hurt him!*

Landing in the backyard, I found Collin staring face to face with a Vampire. His hands were gripped tight around the lawn mower he had been pushing before the Vampire had scared him half to death. It was a female Vampire and she was grinning wickedly at the thought of her next meal.

I began running towards Collin and then watched in horror as the monster leaped for my little brother, fangs bared and ready to bite.

"Collin!" I screamed. He put his hands up to shield his face. Suddenly, his hands burst into flames and the Vampire ran right into them.

Collin's wide shocked eyes kept glancing between his shaking hands and the burning Vampire writhing on the ground in front of him. He was breathing heavily and his breath seemed a little shaky. I ran over and threw my arms around him, relieved that he was unharmed.

"Are you okay?" I asked him.

"I-I think so," he managed to whisper. "What just happened?"

"That was a Vampire," I told him. "And you just killed her."

"What?" he asked in shock.

"I know, right? It's straight out of those horror movies you like so much."

"And my hands…" he said, looking down at his now seemingly normal hands.

"I know," I said, smiling at him. "I can do it too." I lit my hand on fire and showed it to him.

"Whoa," he whispered.

"Go ahead and touch it," I told him. "You're a Fire Elemite, so it won't burn you."

"A what?"

"A Fire Elemite. I'll explain later." Hesitantly, he reached out and touched my hand.

"This is so cool."

Suddenly I realized something. Only one Vampire came and attacked Collin, but there were *two* missing from the fight. If they both followed different scents, then the other one must have gone to…

"Grandpa George," I gasped.

"What?" asked Collin.

"Come on," I told him. Grabbing him by the waist, I jumped into the air and began flying towards the Campton's house. He was surprisingly light and didn't slow me down that much. We made it to the house and I ran inside just in time to see Brian finishing off the Vampire with a little help from Grandpa George's Poison Healer that he always kept in the corner.

"Hey Christa," he greeted me. Then he turned his gaze to Collin. "And you must be Collin. Nice to meet you, I'm Brian."

"Is everyone alright?" I asked.

"We're just fine," answered Sam as he walked in the door with the rest of his family. "They're all dead now. It's fine."

"You mean the Vampires?" Collin asked. "How many were there?"

"Ten," I answered. "There were nine of us fighting them off, but since you killed one, I guess that makes it an even ten on ten."

"Wow," Collin whispered.

"Hey, we're going to head home now," said Tom.

"Oh, yeah," Kyle said. "Thanks so much for all your help."

They went around to everybody to say goodbye and when they got to me, Tom put one of my hands in both of his and shook it.

"Good luck, kiddo," he said. "You're going to need it."

"Oh don't listen to him," Cara told me, shooing him away. She placed one of her hands on each of my shoulders, smiled at me, and said, "You're going to be fine."

Meg came up to me next and gave me a big hug.

"You are so brave," she said. "You're an amazing person, Christa. Just remember that."

"Thank you all so much," I told them. "You guys coming out here to help us meant so much to me and I just want you to know that I appreciate it so much. Thank you."

"Oh, it's alright, Christa," said Tom. "We didn't have any plans today anyways. Now if you had asked us to do this on Super Bowl Sunday, well…" I laughed and Cara and Meg just smiled and shook their heads. Then they all turned and walked out the door, waving goodbye a few last times.

After they had all left, I sat down on the couch and sighed in relief. It was all over. The Vampires were dead and everyone was safe. Sam sat down next to me and put his arm around my shoulders. I smiled at him and he smiled back.

"You were amazing, Christa," he whispered to me, "and so brave."

"I guess all that training paid off, huh?" I said with a smile.

"Yeah, but most Elemites don't master that kind of stuff as fast as you did. I mean you are a really fast learner. I was surprised."

"Thanks Sam."

He smiled at me again and then leaned over to give me a kiss.

Chapter 25

You Knew?

"You know what?" I said to Sam.

"What?" he asked.

"I think it's time we told my mom that Collin and I are Elemites."

"You found out that Collin's an Elemite?" he asked.

"Yeah," I answered. "When I went to go save him from the Vampire, I thought I was too late because the Vampire jumped at him, but then his hands burst into flames and he killed her."

"That's so cool!" Sam exclaimed. "I never expected Collin to get his powers so early."

"Wait a minute. You knew?" I demanded. "You knew he was going to be an Elemite?"

"Well, yeah," he answered. "Remember how I told you that Elemites have a different heartbeat than humans? I noticed that he had the heartbeat of an Elemite, but I didn't want to say anything because I thought it was going to be a few years until he got his powers."

"Well, how come I didn't notice his different heartbeat?"

"You just haven't practiced listening to heartbeats, that's all. You have to know what the difference is if you want to be able to tell the difference between Elemites and humans."

"Okay, but why do you think Collin got his powers so early?"

"I don't know," he admitted. "That might be a question for Grandpa George to answer. He's lived a lot longer and has a lot more experience."

“Alright.” I walked across the room to where Grandpa George was sitting. He was sitting quietly on a comfy chair reading the newspaper as if a Vampire hadn’t just come in here looking to have him as a snack only ten minutes ago. He looked up when he heard me coming and folded the newspaper neatly in his lap.

“Hello, Christa,” he said cheerily. “Is there something you needed?”

“I wanted to ask you a question,” I answered. I explained to him what had happened with Collin and the Vampire and asked if he had any idea why Collin had gotten his powers so early.

“Well, it sounds like it was an instinct to defend himself, so his powers just manifested themselves early in order to fill that instinct.”

“So you mean that the immediate danger triggered his powers so that he could defend himself from the Vampire?”

“That sounds about right.”

“Okay, well, see you later, Grandpa George. I still haven’t really explained to Collin what an Elemite is, so I have to go do that and then I have to go tell my mom that Collin and I are Elemites.”

“Alright. See you later, Christa, and good luck,” he said with a smile on his face and a twinkle in his eye.

I smiled back and walked over to Collin who was admiring Kyle’s Fire Elemite skills.

“Hey, Collin,” I said.

“Yeah, Christa?” he replied.

“It’s time I told you exactly what’s going on.”

“Oh, yeah. Um, can you first explain to me what an Elemite is? People keep using that word.”

"Alright. An Elemite is someone that can control one of the five Elements: Water, Fire, Earth, Air, and Animals. Elemites also have super strength, speed, eyesight, hearing, and sense of smell."

"Whoa," he said. "So I can do that?"

"Yes. You are a Fire Elemite, so you have power over Fire," I told him. Then a thought just occurred to me. "Unless…"

"Unless what?"

"Unless you're like me," I answered. "I can control all five Elements, which is pretty much unheard of."

"That's so awesome! How do we find out if I can do that, too?"

"Come here," I said, walking over to the flower on the windowsill and gesturing for him to follow.

The flower was gorgeous, of course, because Tasha was the one taking care of it. I waved my hand over it and the petals got duller and the stem drooped a little. Then I turned to Collin.

"See if you can make the flower pretty again," I told him.

"You never mentioned power over plants!"

"Power over plants is under the Earth Elemite category. Now just do it."

"How?"

"Just wave your hand over it the way I did and will the plant to get better."

"Alright." He tried it, but nothing happened. After trying a few more times, I decided that he must be just a Fire Elemite.

"I guess you only have Fire Elemite powers," I told him.

"Oh well," he replied. "It's still super awesome and if I had to choose one I would definitely choose power over Fire."

"Well, that's good," I said. "Now there's something else you should know. Dad was an Elemite, too. He was an Animal

Elemite and he wasn't killed in a bear attack. He was killed by a Vampire. He was using the bears to help him fight, but the Vampires got the best of him. The one that killed him was the same one that was leading the Vampire attack today and I killed him."

"So Dad was one of us, too?" he asked, a look of total shock on his face. I nodded. "Wow." We were silent for a few moments before I continued.

"Okay, um, you should also know that there are other magical creatures in this world."

"Really? Like what?"

"There are two types: ones with human-like intelligence that can communicate with us and ones with less-than-human intelligence that cannot communicate with us. Or at least not very well."

"Alright, but what are they?"

"In the first category there are Unicorns, Fairies, Pixies, Mermaids, and Elves. And when I say Elves, I mean like the ones in *Lord of the Rings*, not Santa's elves. In the second category there are Dragons, Giants, and Griffins."

"Sweet! Tell me about Dragons!"

I shook my head. "I'll tell you all about them later. Right now we have to go and tell Mom that we're Elemites. She should be getting home soon and she would freak out if you weren't there when she got back."

"Oh, alright."

"Oh yeah, I almost forgot to tell you. Elemites age like normal people until they get their powers. Then they age half as fast. So in four years, when you're seventeen, you'll look fifteen."

"What? Are you serious?"

"Yep. You see, you got your powers really, really early. Most Elemites don't get them until they're *at least* fifteen. And even that is considered pretty young."

"Now I'm trying to decide whether getting my powers early is awesome or annoying."

I laughed. "It'll be alright, Collin. Anyways, I need to go fly over to the clearing and get my car and then I'll drive it back here and pick you up so we can go tell Mom."

"You're going to do more flying?" he asked. "Why don't you just fly us both to the car and then we can go straight from there to the house?"

"You just want to fly again."

"Duh!"

"Oh, alright. Let's go."

I said goodbye to Sam and the rest of them and then walked out the door with Collin. I grabbed him around the waist and then leaped into the air.

"This is so cool!" he cried, having to yell because of the sound of the air rushing past us.

Apparently he was enjoying himself, so I decided to make the ride even more fun. I did a few twirls and some small dips. I turned this way and that and even did a few dives, pulling out of them long before I thought I needed to because I knew I still wasn't that great of a flier.

We finally made it to the car and I set him down. His hair was windswept and I imagined mine was, too, so I smoothed it down. We got in the car and I drove home.

Our mom got home about a minute after we did.

"Hey guys!" she greeted us. "I'm home! Where's Tracy?"

"She went to a friend's house after school, but she should be home any minute," I answered. As if on cue, Tracy walked through door.

"What's up guys?"

"Collin and I need to talk to you guys," I said.

"Sure honey, what's up?" my mom answered, looking concerned.

"Let's go sit on the couch."

Once we were all seated in the living room, I took a deep breath and started.

"Collin and I have special powers," I said. "We're not like normal humans. In fact, we're not human. We are Elemites. Elemites are like people, only we have power over the Elements: Water, Fire, Earth, Air, and Animals. Each Elemite has power over one of the Elements, that is, except for me. I can control all five. Collin is a Fire Elemite; he has power over Fire. We also have super strength, speed, eyesight, hearing, and sense of smell. We aren't the only ones. Sam and his family are Elemites, too, and so was Dad. He was an Animal Elemite. Collin is special because he got his powers early. Normally Elemites don't get their powers until they're between fifteen and eighteen, but he got his powers today." I finished talking and looked at them, waiting for a response.

"Christa," Tracy began slowly, "Are you okay? Are you sick or something?"

"No, it's true!" Collin told her. "Look!" He held up his hand and it burst into flames. As soon as he did that, Tracy cried out in fright and fell out of the armchair she was sitting in. But Mom just sat there calmly the whole time.

"Mom, you seem strangely calm about all of this," I said. "Are you in shock?"

"No dear, I'm not in shock," she answered. "It's just that, I already know all of this."

"What do you mean you know?" I demanded.

"Your father told me, of course," she said with a smile.

"Now, I didn't know that you could control all the Elements and I didn't know that Collin would be a Fire Elemite or that he would get his powers this early, but I already knew all the rest of it."

"Am I the last one to know everything?" I cried. "I'm the last one to find out that Collin's an Elemite, that dad was an Elemite, and I was even the last one to find out that *I'm* an Elemite. Did you know that it was going to me and Collin that were going to be Elemites?"

She nodded. "With each baby your father listened to its heartbeat and told me whether it would be an Elemite or a human. We decided it would be best if we didn't tell you until you got your powers because otherwise as a child you might have accidentally told the secret without realizing it."

"So, I'm normal, right?" asked Tracy. "I'm not going to randomly have powers someday, too?"

"Yes, Tracy, you are human," answered Mom.

"Okay, well, there's one more thing I have to tell you," I said.

"What is it?"

"Rachel kind of accidentally caught me using my powers, so I told her everything."

"When did this happen?"

"Yesterday."

"You should be more careful where you use your powers," she scolded.

"I was being careful!" I protested. "I was in a clearing in the woods!"

"Either way, it sounds like you need to go visit the Elders."

I nodded, realizing for the first time that I had a long journey ahead of me.

CPSIA information can be obtained at www.ICGtesting.com
Printed in the USA
BVOW070751290512

291138BV00002B/33/P

9 781462 675258